This is a fictional story. All its characters, places and events have been drawn from the author's imagination. Any resemblance to reality is purely coincidental. Except for some trademark names, which were used respectfully and with the sole purpose of giving realism to the story.

© 2017, Rafael Nicolás Pérez
nicolasperez2014y@gmail.com

ISBN-10: 0-9973625-5-3
ISBN-13: 978-0-9973625-5-8

Translation: D.R.
Cover Design: D.R.

First edition: January 2017

# Beautiful Obsession

*Everything for her*

## AUTOR

RAFAEL NICOLÁS PÉREZ

# *Table of contents*

# *Preface*

**MY NAME** is Alex Brown, and the story I'm about to tell you hasn't been told to anyone before. This may be because of how embarrassing or controversial it seems to be or because of my fear of being judged by the society and its prejudices. Whoever discovers what I'm about to reveal will know what to do if they find themselves in the same position, or will, otherwise, be able to judge my actions. Whoever wishes to ignore it will have to toss a coin when the time comes, and hope they made the right decision.

I could make a summary of this story, and thus, take less of the reader's time; but without the full and hidden details, you'll never understand why, after so many years, I've decided to tell my story to the world. If I remember correctly, it all started about five to six years ago, in a bar, where a single look led to everything I am today, and to me being in this hospital.

I remember it all began on a Friday night… How could I forget it!

# Chapter 1

THAT NIGHT... I had a glass of the best whiskey sour you can get at one of the most exclusive bars in New York on my table. I was enjoying the typical Friday fun. Of course, after my workday at a company where I owned twenty percent of the shares. Music, women, dancing, clapping and the same businessmen were always the ones who inhabited the room. That same Friday, I knew it'd be my last night at Knights bar. Just eight months before my wedding: 'My last night!' At least, that's what I thought.

After my third glass of whiskey, she came in. I haven't seen her before, in those three years in which I'd visited the place and sat at the same table, a few feet away from the dance floor, where only the most exclusive and privileged customers could sit...; the VIP area.

She was twirling around a silver colored pole, where she sold her mischievous smile and sensual movements. She exhibited her sensuality at every turn she took. I watched her from my table, located just a few steps away from her work area. As she danced, I noticed she gestured at me, even though there were several entrepreneurs next to me and men all around her. 'She noticed me!' I said to myself, satisfying my ego. When she'd finished, she took a few steps backwards, moving away from the tube and away from my sight, among the vague lights and smoke. Without a doubt, she caught my attention!

After her performance, I decided to stop at the bar and finish my night as I usually did after a Friday night.... Visiting my girlfriend, Lisa and making love to her, as usual. Having sex with her was something we did frequently. On several occasions, we'd have sex without thinking about the date we'd set for our wedding. We'd meet at her apartment to release the carnal desire we felt for each other.

Since the moment I left the bar that night, I couldn't forget that girl's unique style and performance at the pole. 'I want to go back to the bar tonight.' 'But I've never gone to the bar on a Saturday'. 'I have a weird impulse to see her again'. 'I really think I'll go back tonight', I was filled with these thoughts that following Saturday morning.

The day went by and the night came. I showered and got dressed in one of the best suits I had; my best shoes… everything matched my $300 dollar tie; I sprayed one of the best perfumes from my 62 piece collection on my neck; set one of my 46 precious watches on my left wrist and took my BMW 580i's keys. I went to the bar, arriving earlier than usual and in an unusual day for me... everything was done so as not to miss out on the new stripper's performance. Those who knew me at the bar were surprised to see me there, just by the mere fact that it was Saturday. I ordered the usual and sat at the same VIP chair and table. 'Now, I only need her!' I thought, as I savored my first drink of the night.

Hours went by and for as much as I awaited her performance, I only saw the same old faces, except for some entrepreneurs whom I'd never seen before next to me at the VIP area. I ordered my eighth glass of whiskey sour, with two cherries floating in the liquor and ice. The night went by and she wasn't there. 'Is she not working tonight?' I wondered every so often. The show went on and there I was, waiting for her at the bottom of the barrel. As much as I waited and waited, she never appeared on stage, and the bar closed after my tenth glass of whiskey.

When I left, I noticed that the bar across the street, called the Nite bar, was still open. Seeing the people who were still there enjoying the atmosphere through the big windows caught my attention. Holding myself up with my right hand on my car hood and holding the door with my left hand, I looked at the place. 'I would never go to such a dirty little bar like that.' 'Too low class for my taste.' 'Just look at the kind of people who are going in... All drunkards.' 'I can't believe that these people are enjoying that hole.' 'Well, but they're owners of their own lives.' 'I would never go into such a petty canteen', was all I could think of that bar. The early hours were already

11

wreaking havoc in me, after drinking so much alcohol, so I decided to leave.

I was so drunk and disappointed by the time I got home, my body just wanted sleep. Without taking anything off, I passed out in my $ 8,500 dollar bed, after enduring a cat fight in my head; at least that's what I felt after having so much liquor in my body. And it was all for nothing; in the end, she didn't even come on stage.

When I woke up a few hours later, I felt like someone was hammering my head. Luckily, I had all Sunday to rest and try to find a remedy to my discomfort.

Monday morning, I headed to work, after deciding not to go to the gym that morning. Even though my body felt terrible, due to the mistreatment it had gone through two days in a row, something unusual for me, I managed to take my company's reins until noon. While I drove home, my mind tormented me: 'I don't understand why she's still in my head', 'why can't I forget her pirouettes on that damn pole'...

After that night at the bar, every day of the week, I kept her image in my head; I couldn't get her out of my mind even for a second. And days went by. Friday came and this time I hoped I'd have better luck and see her again. That morning, I arrived at the gym for my workout routine, with my friend, Marc.

"How are you, Alex?" he greeted me, as usual.

"Good", I answered somewhat thoughtful.

After we'd spent about twenty minutes in vague conversations and exercise routines.

"What's wrong? You seem to be in a different world, Alex. You don't seem focused on this. We can't continue our routine like this", he pointed out, sitting on the bench that was next to us.

"I'm anxious for time to go by so I can see her again" I stated, placing two 45 pound dumbbells on the floor, with which I exercised my arms, and sitting beside him.

"I don't understand. What the hell do you mean? Truth is you don't look like yourself today, Alex."

"I met a girl last Friday at the bar. Amazing! I'd never seen anything like it. She gave me this unique look. Apparently, she liked me. I already booked my spot at the bar tonight, Blondie; I'd forgotten to tell you about her."

"But you told me last Friday would be your last night at the bar. Are you really thinking about going back there tonight? Didn't you already set a date to marry Lisa?" rubbing my right shoulder, he rose from the bench to face himself… in the mirror; he loved combing his blond hair with his fingers, while staring at himself.

"I know, Marc, but you know me; I want to know why that girl looked at me that way. Look at it this way, Blondie: she could be my last hurrah" I bragged, standing in front of the mirror beside him.

"Truth is, you're never going to change, Alex. You should learn from your brother", he watched his arms in the mirror, and how his muscles changed from white to red and his veins popped, to channel his sweat.

"Then, Blondie, what do you think?" Are you coming with me tonight?"

"You know my wife; so you know I can't, can't even think about it", no doubt, he'd been a master in picking up women, until he decided, at age thirty-three, to take the same path as my brother, John did, and get married. However, I'd always thought marriage wasn't for me, until that week in which I'd set the date to marry my girlfriend, Lisa.

"Then, I'll see you tomorrow", I said as a goodbye, mock-punching him in the liver with my right hand, getting some laughs and walking away from him.

"Poor girl!" I heard him yell when I was leaving the gym.

I went home. I showered, thinking of the new girl and the way she'd looked at me. While I got dressed, I confirmed my reservation, as always, for the bar. I arrived at work and couldn't stop counting the hours, eager for the night to come so I could return to the bar.

It was time to put on the best thing in my closet. I put on a Geoffrey Beene, light blue shirt; matching tie, black shoes and tie of the same brand; Cartier watch, exclusive Versace perfume and got my car keys again to get there early to see her.

After greeting some people I knew, both in the bar and in the VIP section, I ordered the usual; whiskey sour with two cherries. I enjoyed the show and my third glass, while María danced, thereafter, Gina, Rosa, Janeth, Megan and finally, Katy. I knew them all, as in some occasions, I'd shared a drink with several of them. I must confess, it had been different with Gina and Megan, since I got to share... more than drinks with them.

'I can't believe it, she's not coming today either!' 'I could ask about her'. 'You're engaged Alex'. 'You're getting married soon'. 'What's more... you shouldn't even have come today'. 'You swore you'd never come

14

back here', those were some of the thoughts and questions I had roaming in my head, after my sixth glass of whiskey. I felt like my engagement with Lisa had changed my entire perception of life. In a way, I felt guilty for being there, looking for one last night with that girl.

A few minutes later, she, like a goddess, made her entrance. For me, it was like seeing everything that was beautiful in every woman in the world, gathered in a single being. As she danced, I held my glass and I noticed my hand trembled for a few seconds. I couldn't tell if anyone else had noticed my nerves, when I saw her appear among the colored lights that played with her body as she slid on that pole. Her playfulness on that stage was the most impressive and perfect I'd ever seen. In a moment during her performance, she took a few steps forward and began to play with the men who put bills of all kinds in her light fabric panties. While this was happening, she instead of looking at the customers that covered her with money only looked and made gestures to me. It was as if the world around her didn't exist. 'Why is she playing with me?' 'I can't understand her look'. 'Why me?' 'I've never seen her before'. 'She's amazing!' My mind was running at a thousand miles per second. I took another sip form the glass in my hand and, in the blink of an eye... she was next to me. I couldn't believe how fast she'd come so close to me. I hadn't even lowered my glass and she had already begun to play with my $300 tie. She grasped it tightly, pulling me towards her chest. She held my tie with her left hand, while she took one of the two cherries that floated in my glass's liquor and ice with her right, and placed the stick in her mouth, urging me to take the fruit from her mouth with mine. As soon as I held the fruit in my mouth, she let go of my tie, moving away from me, just as she'd arrived.

Those approximately ten minutes she spent with me felt eternal. I thought it'd never end. It was as if everything had happened in slow motion. I awoke from my trance, feeling a few congratulatory pats on my shoulders and back, from some of the people I knew at the VIP. I took a deep breath, trying to recover the one that young girl had stolen.

I stayed in the bar for a few more hours. When I'd already lost count of my drinks, I decided to leave. I opted not to visit my girlfriend that night and finish the day in my apartment. As I drove my car, I couldn't stop thinking of the dancer; I thought of her womanly scent, her sensuality and those eyes that radiated passion.

When I got home, the clock showed 2:00 on Saturday morning and I, being in a better condition than the previous time, poured myself a nightcap, from one of the many whiskey bottles that decorated my little home bar. On the table, next to the room cabinet, I placed my feet, while I enjoyed a few sport videos on the TV, as well as my drink. For as much as I wanted to sleep, I couldn't. 'What's wrong with you, Alex?'. 'Damn it, you're marrying Lisa!' 'Don't get involved.' I could only helplessly think of the agile dancer. For as much as I wanted to shake that memory off my head, it was impossible. Her deep red lips were still in my mind, her shiny honey-colored eyes, her long and silky hair, her jet-black skin and dominant look. In a lucid moment, I returned to reality, noticing that my $300 tie was stained with her red lipstick. 'Did this happen when she was dancing between my legs?' 'Maybe when I was toying with her?', I asked myself, as I held it on the palms of my hands. Instead of feeling angry at the stain, I idolized it, and saved it as a hard-earned trophy. After thinking so much about the dancer, I fell asleep on my $5,000 couch.

Days went by and I only had one thing in mind... seeing her again. 'What's wrong with you, Alex?'. 'You're acting like a child when you're thirty-two.' 'This is wrong', I cursed my strange need to see her. Everything was happening so fast, I wasn't even noticing what was happening within me.

When I was at the gym talking with Marc.

"Did you screw that bar girl, Alex?" asked my blonde friend.

"I haven't even been able to talk to her, Marc. She's very elusive. She's different to the others. With her, I'm another person, I don't even recognize myself. I feel like a newbie with her", I felt sorry for myself.

"I can't believe Alex the charmer is saying something like this. Could it be that the wolf grew old? Hahaha", he smiled in a mocking way, implying I'd lost my conquering skills.

"You know I'll get what I want, before I get married, you can be sure of that, Blondie", I was convinced that it was only a matter of time. I had eight months to achieve my goal and then get away from her.

"Well, we better get on with what we were doing, Alex, I'm tired of you spending all your time talking about that girl and neglecting our routine", he patted me on the back, lifting me off the bench for our leg routine.

# *Chapter 2*

IT'D BEEN almost two months since I'd seen that girl dance for the first time on that blessed pole. My days were no longer the same. My routine had completely changed. My priority now was seeing that girl do her show every Friday; and I put my wedding with Lisa in the back burner. I kept going, as always, to the bar every Friday, even though I promised myself I'd never go back there. I would always sit in the same place and enjoy each of her shows; every twirl she performed, every smile, her way of looking at me and her display on the pole. Just as my encounters with that diva grew closer, so did my wedding with Lisa.

Sometimes, while the new girl danced and when she'd occasionally come to my table, I scanned every part of her, with my eyes, looking for any defect that might remind me that I had a girlfriend whom I was about to marry. I searched for something that made me give up ever seeing her again. For as much as I tried to look for something that would lead to disappointment, I couldn't, despite that small scar that crossed the lower part of her right wrist; she was unique! Almost perfect I'd say. Despite the challenge I'd set for myself, I knew things weren't going as I expected.

'It looks like Marc may be right, there's no wolf left in me', 'maybe I'm afraid of getting what I want', 'I need to show that Blondie, Marc, and myself that I can', I analyzed the pros and cons, as I feared falling for her,

After another week of work, Friday came and, with it, my desire to see her again. She, despite her short time working at that bar, had become the diva of the place. Men idolized her; it was she everyone wanted to see. Nobody wanted to miss her show. Most of them shouted crazily when they saw her come on stage, each time with something new. I, however, began to feel jealous of each of the men who rested his eyes on her. I couldn't explain my jealousy, as even though she often danced for me, we'd never even had a conversation. I didn't even know how her voice sounded like; what's more, she sometimes dirtied my expensive tie and sometimes, my shirt.

After combining my white shirt with my tie; putting on dark gray pants and Aldo shoes and my Movado wrist watch; I sprayed on some perfume, grabbed my car keys, and there I was again… waiting for her. 'Tonight, at least, get her name, Alex.' According to my calculations, she'd be on soon. Behold the reason for all my troubles: her blessed gaze! I kept repeating to myself, over and over again —I whispered. Suddenly, she started walking towards my table, after not having done so in the last two weeks. She was getting closer, I could see her move closer, and without being able to control my emotions, I simply waited for her. When she arrived, she ran her soft hands through my hair, playing a bit with her fingers, lost in my black, wavy hair. Her honey-colored eyes, ran into my green eyes, and our gazes met. As she placed her left foot on one side of my seat, for a moment, she pulled my head towards her naked chest. I could feel the youth of her breasts in my face. I got carried away by her seduction. She moved my head away from her chest, releasing my hair, to then move her hand down my neck, stroking me lightly with her fingernails and fingertips. While she danced for me, she left a napkin in my shirt pocket, ending her performance, and at the same time, my anxiety. Taking a few steps backwards, I lost sight of her, like every Friday, in the rainbow of lights and smoke curtain, leaving me breathless. This time, she went further than previous times, by leaving that napkin in my shirt pocket. 'I'm not sure if I'm just a part of her show, or if she thinks I'm different than the other customers...' I read what was written in the napkin, after a good and long gulp: 'Private No. 3 in 20 minutes.' Ten minutes had passed before I'd read her note. Surreptitiously, I went to the private indicated on that napkin. Upon arrival, my gaze sought her insistently. It had been 27 minutes and I was still standing there, feeling really stupid, and looking everywhere. I felt like a young child, thinking that Santa Claus would come down the chimney with my bike in hand. At the 30th minute, I gave up on that alleged meeting. I went into the bathroom next to private No. 3, and fixed my shirt and tie. I left the bathroom five minutes later. I had just taken a few steps out of the bathroom when I felt a woman's hand stroking my hair. Turning my head, wanting to see who it was, another hand pulled my tie... 'It's her!'. With a single tug, she led me to the previously agreed private. I couldn't believe this was happening! Very gently, she pulled me towards one of the walls of the private. Pushing her body into mine, she again played with my hair; she insinuated kissing my mouth, without ever touching my lips. Pulling my tie, she took my body to the white leather couch. My senses were tingling and my white skin turned red, I didn't know if it was due to the yanks she was giving me or the nerves overwhelming me. She maintained her seduction game and domination over me. She slipped both hands through my shirt and in the midst of her dancing; she started opening one by one, each of its buttons, until she freed the last one. A minute later, she was loosening my belt buckle, and thus, managing to free what was left of my shirt tucked into my pants. She spreads open my shirt, leaving my chest and abdomen in sight. With her hands, she stroked my well exercised body; she placed her hands on my worked out stomach, forming a heart around my navel, which, slowly, she kissed. I, surprised, enjoyed the moment. Ten minutes went by, and she owned each second of them. Again, she pretended to kiss my mouth and, in a desperate attempt, I tried to reach her lips, but she knew how to escape mine. In her flight, she ended up on my left ear and, slowly, slipped her lips down my neck. In the last fifteen minutes, I hadn't been able to hear her say a single word. She only continued with her power game. Taking off a transparent blouse and showing a deep cleavage, she danced sitting on my penis, erect and ready to burst. Through her continuous movements, I managed to touch her breasts with my lips for a few seconds. I felt their stiffness. Her nipples were as sharp and appetizing as I could imagine. At some point... I think driven by my nerves or perhaps my despair, I asked:

"May I know your name?" and that was the first time I heard her voice.

Lifting my chin with her left hand to look into my eyes, her mouth opened to gently, sensually and safely say:

"Silence, relax! Just enjoy the moment! Bad boy!"

At the end of her act, after twenty minutes of submitting me to her erotic games, everything was over and it went no further than being a private function. She walked away, with the intention of leaving me there. At that moment, I pulled one of her arms, stopping her when she was about to cross the door frame. I placed a $100 bill in her hands and asked again:

"Now, can I get your name?"

She took the money, fixing her gaze on mine; then, she pulled out a lipstick from her purse. She wrote something on the bill, resting it on my back, to then leave it in my pants' left pocket. She brought me towards her by pulling on both my pockets accompanied by a gentle kiss on my lips.

"Why do you need to ask so many questions?" she whispered, crossing the door and giving me the side glance that had once made me return to the bar.

She left, leaving her womanly scent on me. I was alone and crushed, with my third tie dirty with lipstick and my second shirt in the same condition. After receiving a private dance I hadn't expected, I couldn't stand the pain in my genitals. I simply felt an intense desire to have sex with a woman. After seeing her leave, it was clear it wouldn't be her. 'I'm just a game.' 'She's surely just like the others', I thought, very disappointed in her. I didn't understand why the hell I wanted it to be different with me, if my intention had always been to fuck her and leave her as soon as possible.

I then decided to visit my girlfriend, Lisa. But I couldn't go as the erotic dancer had left me, all messy and with dirty clothes. So first, I went to my apartment. I showered and changed clothes in record time. As I drove, I called my girlfriend, letting her know I was on my way to visit her.

When I knocked on her door, she appeared and my sexual desire increased upon seeing her. She was wearing a white button-down shirt, which she'd tied in a knot near her belly button; white panties, very clung to her buttocks; her hair, short and blond, was dripping water onto her shoulders, and her body smelled like that perfume I liked.

I'd never felt so much desire to make love to my girlfriend, as I did that night. She asked, as usual, if I wanted a drink before bed. I didn't give her time to say anything else, and grabbing her butt, I carried her to one of the living room walls. Kissing her lips, I removed each of the buttons on her blouse, until I got to the knot. Right then, I noticed the difference between thirty-five year old breasts and those of a twenty-something year old. I took one of her breasts into my mouth and pulled her nipple with my lips several times. I placed my right hand around her waist, pulling her tightly, resting her on my body; I kissed her neck, running my fingers through her wet hair. I saw the blouse fall on the floor, after I'd abruptly pulled it off her with my hands, leaving her with a single garment on her body... her white panties. I took both her legs, making her ride her slender body on my waist. With my pants and my underwear already rolling on the ground, and after shaking them off several times with my legs, I slid her panties to a side and put my penis into her vagina, making her moan with pleasure, while kissing her moistened lips. Then I took her to the bed, taking small steps, where I threw her in despair. I clung to her slender body, kissing her all over, without leaving a single space un-kissed, and after satiating my desire, more than hers, we both rested, exhausted. At dawn, she asked for more and I delivered; so we had sex again.

After making love the second time:

"What happened, love?!" apparently, my way of making love that night had surprised her.

"I don't understand the question, Lisa!" I answered, very exhausted and staring at the ceiling.

"Your performance... I don't know, it was different this time. It wasn't like you! I felt you were a bit aggressive... but I liked it", she whispered, laying on the bed as tired as I was.

"Do you really think so, love?!"

"I loved it!" she sighed, with a satisfied look, stroking my chest with her right hand.

As I was driving back home, I remembered that bill in the pocket of the pants I'd changed before going to my girlfriend's house. I stepped on the accelerator and soon after, I was opening my apartment door. Eager to see what was written on the forgotten bill, I grabbed my pants desperately. After taking the money, on one side, it said "Alisha" and on the other; "ten minutes in the parking lot." "I can't believe I'm reading this!" "Why didn't I look before?" I thought, while squeezing the $100 bill, taking a few steps in frustration, then tore it into pieces.

That Saturday, I could only regret what couldn't be. All that flood of passion that happened between Lisa and me, and now I was thinking it could've been with the new girl; although, I have to confess that everything I did to my fiancée was inspired by the stripper. 'I don't know what happened!' 'That man who made love to Lisa wasn't me'. 'That's why she had those questions'. 'It seems incredible it was all inspired by that girl.' 'But, why is this happening with her?' 'I have barely seen her', I thought, not being able to understand my emotions.

I, who always took the initiative with women; now, felt manipulated by a girl in her early twenties. 'I've never felt this way'. 'Why her? Why now? Only months before my wedding?' My head no longer had any lucidity, since I'd met the erotic dancer. I only thought of her and very little of my fiancée. Being with that woman became a challenge; I knew it would be my last adventure before marrying Lisa. Unexpectedly, it was all becoming a very dangerous game. I'd never invested so much time into getting a woman to give me a night of pleasure. With her, I couldn't even talk for five minutes straight.

*Chapter 3*

FRIDAY came again. This time, I wouldn't be able to see her, due to a prior commitment. I had to attend Luisa's party, my future sister-in-law, who was turning nineteen on that same day. This time, I dressed more casually, as I wouldn't be going to the bar that night, even though I was dying to see her; now, I knew her name. However, that was a luxury I couldn't afford.

That night, I wore jeans, Prada belt and shoes, Bulova watch and a tight Gucci t-shirt. I grabbed my keys, and this time, I opted for my red sports Porsche with black leather seats. I went to the club where Luisa's birthday party would take place.

The clock showed 8:00 pm, and I kept on thinking about where I wanted to drive my car, instead of the route I was taking. But at the same time, I thought that I couldn't fail Luisa as well as her entire family. I'd promised my sister in law and my girlfriend that I'd be there. My family would also go to the celebration, except for my brother John.

It was shortly after 9:00 pm, and I could only think about the young girl and the time she'd come on stage. 'You're in a family atmosphere, Alex.' 'What's wrong with you, my God?'. 'Control yourself, control your mind!'. 'Don't get carried away by temptation', I thought, until I heard my name.

"Alex, come over! We're taking pictures with my sister! Alex!!!"

"Ok, Lisa, I'm coming", I walked straight to her, leaving my thoughts behind.

Another hour went by, and even though I was there, I didn't feel like myself. My mind was still at the bar with the agile dancer. 'It's almost time for her show', I kept on repeating to myself, looking at my watch over and over again. I couldn't help thinking about her, and about what could've happened the night I left her waiting at the bar parking lot.

Suddenly, I thought of something, to leave the bar and go see her, at least for a few minutes, and return to the celebration within an hour. I pretended to take a call on my phone, standing very close to my fiancée.

"Hey John", I said, sideways glancing at my girlfriend.

"...?"

"I can't right now; I'm at my sister-in-law, Luisa's birthday, remember?" I pretended to answer to my brother.

"...?"

"Bye, John!" I said, hanging up the call, and putting my phone in my pocket.

"Was it John?", asked Lisa casually.

"Yes, it was him love. He needs some papers he left in my office.

"He's not coming to my sister's party?"

"I don't think he can, Lisa", I hugged her waist and kissed her cheek.

"Are those papers really important, love?"

"Apparently, yes."

I took advantage of a call that came right at that moment, from my friend Marc. I picked up the phone, rejected it, and pretended that I took it.

"There you are again brother."

"Tell him to pick them up here, and that way he can also come to the party", she completely ignored my trick.

"Give me a minute love, I'll be right back. Let me talk to him", I said taking a few steps away from her.

"What happened, Alex? Is John coming or not?"

"Honey, I have to take those papers to him. He's saying they're very important. And that's also why he can't come."

"But, you can't go, Alex!" she dug her eyes on mine, like a menacing dagger.

"I'll only drop off the documents and will return within the hour, love. It's still early! Tell your sister I'll be back", I whispered, kissing her on the lips and walking away from her.

"Please, Alex! You can't leave!" She shouted when she saw me walking away, leaving her behind.

"I'll be right back! My parents should be arriving soon; tell them, please, that I'll be right back", I shouted back, turning my head and throwing her a kiss.

I always knew my brother wouldn't attend my future sister-in-law's party. Something the others ignored. That's why I thought about that reason to leave.

My watch now said 10:20 pm and I was able to buy at least one hour with my lies and acting. 'What are you getting into, Alex?'. 'This isn't you.' 'What's happening with you and that girl?', I thought as I walked to my car. Without wasting any more time, I got in my Porsche and headed straight to the bar. I didn't have enough time to get to my apartment and change, so I simply rushed there. When I reached the bar, my clock said 10:42 pm. 'Just in time!' I thought, entering the establishment.

Her show started around 11:00 pm. I still had some time to see her again. This time, I didn't care about what table I'd sit at, as I didn't have much time and I still needed to return to the party, after seeing her for a few minutes.

She appeared and I couldn't believe my eyes. Her arrival to the pole was very different this time from previous ones. From a single jump, and with a single hand, she spun her body on it. 'Apparently, she's noticed I'm here!', I said to myself as I watched the show. Inside, I wanted her to come to my table that night; but at the same time I begged God that she wouldn't. My pleas were in vain. In a second, she was by my side. I could tell because of her perfume. How could I forget her womanly scent? She began to seduce me, as always. She played with my hair, and insinuated her beautiful body on mine.

That night, I wasn't wearing one of my elegant shirts or expensive ties. I wasn't in my VIP spot either, which is why her games would be different. At one point in her performance, she circled my seat, standing behind me. She placed her soft, delicate hands on my chest, wrapping her arms above my shoulders, and whispered in my ear:

"You didn't show up that night."

At that time, I tried to turn around and apologize, but it was impossible. She had complete control over the situation and whispered again:

"Relax! Bad boy!"

She continued with her performance, with both her hands on my shirt, brushing her lips against one of my ears. She took a few steps following the beat of the music and then she was again in front of me, looking at me with those hazel eyes. She knew she had me, she could do anything with me. Placing a hand on my chest, she moved her body sensually, as she danced to her second song. Right at that moment, my phone's constant ringing made me take it out of my pocket; she, upon seeing the phone in my hand, took it gently and rejected the call, lowered its volume to vibrate; later leaving it on the table beside my drink. She did all of this without missing a beat. I thought the missed call could be Lisa. Minutes later, slowly, the phone began to move on the table, from side to side, due to the vibration. I grabbed it as I could; I wanted to check who was calling and right there, it was my fiancée. Suddenly, she took it away from me again; this time, turning it off completely.

"I don't want any distractions! Bad boy!" she whispered again in my ear.

Again, my phone was on the table, next to my glass. Thereafter, she took control of the situation and, after a few minutes, her power over me ended.

"See you soon", she said walking away, giving me that look; leaving a kiss between my cheek and lips.

I didn't understand what she meant by that. I didn't even have time to look for an answer, just as she had showed up; she had disappeared; vanishing among the lights, people and smoke. I again grabbed my phone. It was 11:23pm. The only thing I could think about as I left my table... was getting to Luisa's party as soon as possible. I rushed to turn on my car. I turned on my phone on my way to the Porsche and the first thing I saw on the screen was five missed calls... all of my fiancée. I kept walking hurriedly. My mind and reasoning were torn between calling my girlfriend or not. I didn't want to waste time thinking about what to do, so I chose to call her on my way back to the party.

To my surprise, my phone vibrated in my hand; again, Lisa's name showed up on the screen. I had no excuse at the time to justify my delay. So I let it vibrate and then, put it in my right pocket. When I placed it in there, I felt something very soft against my fingers. When I removed it, I noticed it was a bar napkin. In it, she'd written with lipstick. 'Parking lot in twenty...' I stopped upon reaching my car. My head was even more befuddled after reading that. My decision had to be quick, as I didn't have much time. I didn't know whether to call my girlfriend and lose the chance of seeing the young girl, or seizing the moment with her and opting for a fight with my fiancée. 'However, a fight with Lisa is already a fact', I analyzed my options, holding the napkin in my hands. After some thought, I made my decision...; after five minutes of the twenty the dancer had proposed, I arrived at the parking lot. There was my human goddess, about to get into the car of one of her dancer colleagues, Rosa. A face familiar to me. Young Alisha was dressed as I'd never seen her; in a wine-red dress, belted with a black belt that hugged her waist; her black hair in a single braid that rested over her left shoulder and ended on her navel; black stilettos; carmine red lipstick, matching her dress and black bag, that hung from her shoulder. "You look beautiful!" I said, after shouting her name and seeing her face turn to see me. Suddenly, I saw her friend kiss her on the cheek and start her car.

'I can't believe it!', 'she's staying!'. 'What does this girl want with me?' 'Why am I nervous?' 'What power does she have over me?' These were some of the questions that haunted my head, while she said goodbye to the redhead. She walked towards me, imposingly. Her eyes were bright, but dominant; her walk, elegant. I looked at her and couldn't believe that was the same girl who'd dance on that pole every Friday and the only one guilty of what was eating me inside. 'Whoever saw her wouldn't be able to tell what she could do on a pole.' 'Why is she looking at me like that?' 'Why are my hands sweaty?' 'What's happening to me?' She's just a dancer, Alex.' 'You know you can't fall in love!'. I knew she was by my side because of her perfume, her scent was unique. I could distinguish her between a thousand women. When she was standing in front of me, I was able to figure out her height based on mine: '5ft 8 inches without heels', 'I must be two inches taller than her', I thought instantly. She gave me a kiss that started on my cheek and ended on the corner of my mouth. The same she'd given me before. It was as if she was beginning to see me in a different way.

"Where's your car?" her question was sensual, and yet authoritative.

"Across the street", my nerves upon answering her was noticeable. I still couldn't assimilate what was happening.

"Let's go!" she was sure I'd follow her command.

"Where are we going?"

"Why do you always have to ask so many questions? Just take me to your car", she was playing with her lips, giving me that imposing look and walking away from that place.

As we walked, I didn't dare ask anything else; I simply followed her elegant steps.

"Which one's your car?" she asked, looking at both sides, standing on the sidewalk.

"It's the red Porsche, across the street" I attempted to impress her with it; she didn't even flinch. Apparently, it wasn't the first one she'd seen.

"Let's go!" she stated, treating me like a small child, who she could manipulate.

The other men, who were leaving the bar, looked at me with her and whispered among them... I don't know what... maybe about the two of us, I assumed. It felt good to walk next to her and have the others see me. I felt as if she'd been the prize of a bet among the men who attended that bar and, in the end, I had won.

While I drove the car, she gave me directions, and at the same time my phone wouldn't stop vibrating in my pocket. I didn't dare take it out for obvious reasons:

1) I could already imagine who was calling.

2) I didn't want the girl next to me to notice.

3) She could've even thrown it out the window.

Based on my perception, she hadn't noticed that my phone was vibrating... how mistaken I was!

"If you get it I'll get off the car!" she stated, turning her head to the left, making me notice that my phone was vibrating and that she knew.

I kept driving and she only opened her mouth to state her stand, tell me where to turn, and nothing else. 'But, what does this girl think?' 'I don't know why I don't draw the strength to impose myself'. 'Take control of the situation.' 'Could it be due to fear of not seeing her again?'. 'Of losing her attention?' 'I've always been the one to set the game rules!' 'Why am I letting myself be manipulated?' 'She's just a spoilt girl.' 'I think she needs some spanking to learn how to respect me!' 'You know you're not the only one, Alex.' 'Just fuck her and get away from her.'

"Stop!" she yelled suddenly.

She was still controlling me. Even if I tried to impose my power, I couldn't. I didn't have the courage... perhaps for fear of losing what wasn't even mine. And to all this, my phone wouldn't stop vibrating. I got off the car and went to her side to open her door like a gentleman:

"Are you turning it off or am I?" she whispered, giving me an ultimatum with that sexy yet powerful look.

"What's wrong with her?" "Does she think I'm a puppet she can handle at will.' 'She could use a few spanks". "Doesn't she know I always get what I want?" "That it's easy for me to walk away once I get what I want?" I was forced to turn it off completely.

We entered a building, and after going up, I don't know how many steps, we reached the third floor. It wasn't luxurious, but it was large and nicely decorated. I kept very quiet, due to her sudden attitude changes. I waited for her to say something, before uttering a word. The girl had very few words, but when she used them, it was to take control. 'I'm in a house I don't know, with a powerful woman'. 'What am I after following her orders?' 'Why can't I take control?'. 'You're about to get married, Alex.' I looked around the apartment, surprised and wondering what I was looking for there just months before my wedding.

"You live here?" I asked, looking at the place.

"Yes, this is where I live."

"Your apartment is very nice!" it wasn't fancy, but it was clean and comfortable; her frames match the violet of her walls and her white curtains. My nerves made me stumble on the purple sofa; it was slightly darker than the walls, it looked very welcoming, I'd say perfect! For what my thoughts demanded at the time.

"Thank you", her answers were always very sharp, without much detail. She seemed to fear my questions.

"Why did you bring me here, Alisha?" my nerves reminded me of my first time. As if still, at my age, I was a rookie with women.

"Just relax! Bad boy!" I only heard her whisper this, and then in a second, she was on top of me, running her left hand through my hair and neck. With her right hand, she led me to the bathroom, softly kissing my neck. As we walked… shoes, socks, pants and belt were left behind. Her dress slid off her body, and rolled to the ground, next to her black heels, revealing the most perfect body I'd ever seen. She was only wearing a red thong that tightly hugged her buttocks. At one point, I tried getting my shirt off, but she stopped me from doing it, pushing me into the tub. She turned on the shower, at a moderate temperature, wetting her body and mine completely. Once we were both inside and soaking wet… desire, passion and madness. For the first time, she kissed my lips tightly. She, but me, without reaching pain. Instead, it increased my pleasure and desire for her. As always, she controlled the situation. I got carried away and enjoyed what I was feeling at the time. Still with my wet boxers on and her wet panties, my erect penis grazed her vagina. With my fingertips, I played with one of her nipples, increasing its size to the maximum. She gently and delicately lowered her left hand, putting it inside my underpants, and taking my penis which was ready to burst; and after taking off my boxers, she finally took off my soaking wet shirt; and I, desperately, finally tore off her underwear. Now we could freely touch all of our bodies. The inner fire of her body and mine increased to one hundred percent, despite the water falling on us. I pushed her against the wall, placing my hands on her buttocks and pressing my sex to hers, as my mouth sucked on her left breast, which was as tight as her buttocks. Rubbing my penis on her vagina increased the tension. Just then, I felt in control of the situation for the first time. My control over her... lasted for as long as a cotton candy would last in a child's mouth at a fair, as in an unexpected turn, one of those she knew so well, the one who had his back against the wall was me; she had regained control. She grabbed my hands, crossing them above my head and holding them against the wall, until she tied them to the shower head with my wet shirt. She bit my lower lip and slid gently down my chest, reaching my navel, where she placed a kiss that shook me inside. After a few seconds, slowly, she went down to my penis, and taking it with her left hand sucked it several times with her mouth. She knew what she was doing with her lips and tongue. While she enjoyed it, I, however, was dying of pleasure. She could tell, due to my moans when she twisted her body, and because of her right hand which was on my heart. She could feel my chest beating fast and knew it wasn't normal; she also knew she had me where she wanted and took advantage of it. Suddenly, she stopped precisely when I needed her to, so I wouldn't leave my semen in her mouth. She left my penis to again slide up my body and release her already wet hair from the braid. Seeing her wet loose hair while I was tied up, and watching her play with the water, moving her hair from side to side, excited me beyond belief. She stopped playing and went for my lips; but before then, she had looked at me in the eyes, as if she wanted to make sure I was still under her power. She played with my lips and hers. Suddenly… her tongue and mine met. My tied hands stopped me from touching her when I wanted to. I could've easily broken free, but I didn't... I liked feeling overpowered by her. Her lips began to run over my neck, stopping at my left nipple, biting it with subtlety. Then she left it to get a condom. After placing it on my erect penis, she released my hands and I immediately grabbed her by the waist, imprisoning her body against mine and introduced my penis into her vagina. As we moved, she turned me around and now she was against the wall. As she kissed me, nibbling me, she raised her body on my waist, crossing her legs behind my back and placing her hands around my neck. The cries of pleasure came in waves. I squeezed her buttocks with my hands and she, feeling the strength of my fingers, clung to my back, almost clawing and biting my left shoulder, asking me not to stop over and over again. She bit my lips with more strength than before, it was like one wanted to eat the other. We stumbled all over the bathroom walls and the windows of her already fogged sliding doors. We both shouted one last time, a few seconds apart; and merged into one as our bodies shriveled. We were overcome by pleasure, and the water kept falling on our thick and sweaty skin. At the end of all that overflow of passion and madness, I was glued to her body, wishing to spend the last hours of the morning with her. For a moment, I thought she wanted the same thing; until, suddenly, when she shook her body from mine and to my surprise... broke the sweet moment after sex:

"You need to leave!" she said, adding nothing else.

"Why?" my disappointment was noticeable, when I heard her say that as she left the bathtub.

"Just leave and don't ask any questions", she repeated, without any explanation.

"Why are you like this with me?"

"I told you not to ask any questions. Just leave, please!" she said again, wrapping her body in a pink towel.

"Don't you at least want to know my name?" I was trying to get more time with her.

"I know it… Alex!" she surprised me by saying my name.

"And how did you know it?"

"Every girl at the bar knows your name. Especially the ones you've already fucked", she seemed to know everything about me. More than I thought.

"Who's saying that…?" I was trying to deny it so she wouldn't think badly of me.

"You don't need to give me any explanations", she stated, putting on white pajama pants and a white blouse, made of a transparent silk that showed me her nipples, which seemed to be yelling at me to stay.

"It's just that... what they've told you, it's not true."

"Just leave, Alex."

"I imagine you're not the sort of girl to accept chocolates, right? Just give me a second and I'll look for my wallet in my pants and give you some money", I wanted to pay her for a night of sweat and pleasure.

"Why do you always want to show off your money? I didn't bring you to my house for money and I haven't asked for it. You rich people, you always think you can buy everything with money", apparently my offer had really bothered her. It was as if my attitude somehow offended her.

"I'm sorry! Then..." Will I see you tomorrow?" I asked, buttoning my pants.

"It's already tomorrow! If you look at your $ 3,500 watch, you'll notice."

"I could see you on Sunday, Monday or perhaps Tuesday. Just tell me the day", I couldn't even understand why I insisted on seeing her again.

'Stop insisting, Alex, just forget about her. You got what you wanted, now go. You no longer need to take all that spoilt attitude and orders', I told myself.

"You'll see me whenever you go to the bar" she was still being more sarcastic than funny.

"But, why not tomorrow?"

"There's no tomorrow for me, only today. Now leave! It's late and I need to rest. I feel very tired", she said, putting my shirt on my chest.

"But, it's still wet. Why don't we have sex again until my clothes dry?" I still wanted to stay by her side, despite her insistence on me leaving her apartment.

"Because it'll only be when I decide, however I decide, and wherever I decide", she said strongly, as she watched me determinedly.

'Damn, Alex, just go. You don't have to put up with her insolence and childishness' I repeated to myself again.

"Why does your attitude change? Sometimes sweet and other times... so aggressive. May I know your age?" I asked, because I thought she was about 22 or 23; but at her age, I didn't understand how she could be so sure of herself.

"Just go! Take this, put this on and go already...!" this time, her voice was stronger.

"But it's a woman's shirt!" I said, as she pushed my body with her left hand on my chest.

When I was crossing the living room, I noticed something I hadn't when I'd come in... a small bookshelf on one of her walls. One book in particular caught my attention from the many she had there... '50 Shades of Grey'. Apparently, it was the one she was reading at the time, as it looked out of place on the shelf. I was never fond of reading, but due to its popularity, I ended up going to the movies to see that film. That already gave me a lot to think about her, when I remembered she tied my hands to the bathroom shower. I had no more time for questions. At the end, I ended up with her shirt and more confused than before.

'I don't understand why she plays with me like that'. 'As if I were a small child.' 'First, she's sweet, then bitter'. 'I don't understand her'. 'She knows everything about me, based on her words'. 'Why take her impositions?' 'She's nothing but a spoilt child, Alex'. 'But as beautiful as the goddesses'. 'Her dark skin, those eyes that shine with their own light, her hair and her seductive ways.' 'Damn you, Alisha! What the hell are you doing to me?'

## Chapter 4

**AS I DROVE,** I couldn't help thinking about everything that had happened; until reality hit my mind... 'My God, Luisa and her party!' 'What am I going to tell my girlfriend?'. 'How do I get out of this?' I turned on my phone; among the missed calls and messages, a total of twenty-six, I found a couple of calls from her sister, Luisa, and two from my sister, Sara. 'Well, tomorrow I'll have to make up an excuse.' I had no other choice.

I got to my apartment and made myself a strong drink. As I drank it, I tried to settle my feelings. 'I'm months away from getting married'. 'Why am I getting involved in this thing that keeps me from thinking clearly?' 'And which will surely lead to nothing good'. 'It'll be better to stay away from that girl once and for all.' 'Yes that'll be best'. 'In the end I already got what I wanted'. 'I think it'll be easier to get away from her now'. 'I've done it before, why should now be any different?'

Again, a call from my phone yanked me back to reality. 'There she is again, it's Lisa!' 'But I can't answer without a plan drawn up'. 'I need to think of something'. 'I'll think of something tomorrow!' Thinking on what had happened with the stripper, I fell asleep, hugging her shirt. At around 11:00 on Saturday morning, I hung it up with my trophies... sorry, my lipstick-stained ties and shirts.

Later, I went to my fiancée's house. I took several deep breaths, before knocking on her door and not due to the fatigue of climbing two floors, but because of what was coming. Entrusting myself to God... I rang her doorbell twice, before she came out.

"Hi, honey!" I said, apparently shamelessly.

"How dare you call me honey, after what you did to me last night, Alex?" she stated, laying her hands on my chest and pushing me into the hallway outside her door.

"But honey, let me explain!" To my luck, women never want explanations; they prefer to draw their own conclusions. She interrupted me, and gave me information I was unaware of.

"I called John and he told me you never went. Where were you all this time? Why did you really leave?" She asked persistently, still screaming.

Her way of fighting, without a pause, was giving me time to think. While she screamed, I thought of my brother. 'It was a mistake not calling John'. I didn't know what he'd said in that call. I was risking everything with the answer I'd give.

"You know well, I left to take the papers to my brother."

"Well, I don't believe you. I asked him if you went to see him. And what do you think he answered? Clearly, he told me you never showed up. What explanation do you have for that?" Her anger, instead of decreasing, grew like foam.

"Babe, if only you talk, I can't explain. Let me in and I'll tell you, Lisa", I begged, trying to take her hands.

"I'll listen, but here at the door, because your entry into my house will depend on how much I can believe your story", she yelled angrily and pushed my body again into the building hallway.

Occasionally, I'd see a neighbor poke his head out, trying to see what all the fuss was about.

"As you know, I went to the office to get some papers. As I was driving to John's house, a young woman crossed in front of me and I ran her over… it wasn't serious, but I had to take her to the hospital, waited until she felt better so I could leave knowing she'd be fine. When I left, I paid her bill and left her some money. If you look at my eyes, you'll be able to notice I haven't slept at all", I explained, without finding a better excuse to give her, and in a low voice as some neighbors had woken up.

"And what about my calls and texts to your phone?" she asked, now in a softer tone.

"I'm getting to that, honey… as is typical of me, this is the third phone I lost, I dropped it in the water when I was washing my hands and face at the hospital bathroom. You know I'm very clumsy with that", I placed my wet phone in her hands as well as some random papers.

"Love, are you telling me the truth...?" she asked, loosening her cheeks and changing her face's strong expression for a more peaceful one.

"I swear, honey! You know I wouldn't lie to you with something as serious as that. Actually, lend me your phone so I can call John so he won't worry about your calls; and so I can get him the papers at once", I stroke her cheeks and took her waist.

"Ok, love. Remember you need to apologize to my sister Luisa" she said, handing me her cellphone and, apparently, accepting my arguments.

"Of course, Lisa!" I kissed her lips and got as far away from her as I could, walking all the way down the hallway. I needed to talk to John and learn all the details of his conversation with Lisa; tell him what had happened and how I had solved everything.

In my conversation with him, I never took my eyes off my girlfriend, in case she ever thought of walking closer to me.

"I can't believe the old wet phone trick still works for you, haha!" said my brother, laughing.

"I had no other choice than to dump it in water this morning, until I drowned it, to get out of all this."

"Well, if the strategy still works, the better. Let's meet up today and you can tell me everything in detail. I want to know everything, what do you think?"

"Ok. I'll tell Lisa you're coming to get the papers; in the meantime, I'll try to make her even more convinced by what I told her."

"Good. I'm on my way."

As I waited for John, I approached my girlfriend and, as I was returning her phone, she insisted that I should contact her sister, Luisa; but, at that moment, I had a different priority. I interrupted her insistence with small, yet very passionate kisses, pushing her body into the apartment. From the living room, we went into her bathroom and she, though a bit surly, finally got carried away and all our clothes were left behind, only leaving the gray blouse covering her body. I turned on the shower. Clearly, I had control of everything that was happening between us. Though with a few variations, everything was very similar to what I'd gone through with the stripper; only this time... it was me and my rules.

I took her to the limit when I reached her vagina after running through her body; with my lips I made her moan with pleasure. Her moans increased when, at the same time, I pressed her buttocks with my hands. Very softly, I kissed her clitoris, leading her to an emotional state I hadn't seen in her for a long time. She pushed my head towards her vagina with her hands, as she twisted her body with desire. I softly run up her body, until our sexes were together, without penetration. After stripping her off her soaked blouse, I clumsily tried to tie her hands to the shower head... I gave up, letting it fall to the floor. As I ran my lips down her body, I stopped for a second to tenderly bite her left shoulder. Kissing one of her breasts, I bit her nipple very softly. At some point, I looked for Alisha's long hair, completely forgetting how short my girlfriend's hair was. She couldn't stand the pressure anymore and asked to have my penis in her. I climbed her on my waist, waiting for her to cross her legs behind my back and bite my shoulder. Her legs were suspended on my arms with her hands around my neck. As a wave of warm water moistened us, we moistened our sexes, ejaculating at the same time and with the same sigh of relief, our bodies were left exhausted.

After having had sex with Lisa in that way, she simply looked into my eyes with a surprised look on her face and without inquiring about anything that had happened; she asked a thousand questions with her eyes. She made coffee, and as we were drinking it, she called her sister and it was my time to apologize, with the same excuse I'd given her. Then, John arrived, and saying goodbye to my girlfriend, we went to a nearby restaurant. His cheeky smile made me ask:

"What are you laughing about, John?"

"Sorry brother... but I can't believe Lisa is still buying that wet phone story, hahaha! How many times have you told it? What, four, five, six times? How many has it been?... hahaha!" his smile was somewhat mocking.

"Don't exaggerate. This is the third time. I have to go buy another one as soon as we leave."

"Tell me everything about the new victim of your follies and mysteries, mere months before your wedding. You really are crazy, Alex!" John saw something in my behavior I didn't want to see and which I kept asking myself since I met her.

"That's the thing, John. This time, she's the one with follies and mysteries. I don't understand her deal. If you saw her... she's a goddess! Her dark skin, her eyes and that perfect body. She's unique, brother!"

"But, I imagine this is just one of your whims, Alex, and that it won't go further than this."

"The truth is, I don't know. It's like she has some power over me. Nothing like this had ever happened to me."

"From what I hear, you're getting too deep into this girl, don't you think, Alex?" it was as if he was reading my mind.

"I don't know, John; perhaps you're right."

"Where did you meet her? Where does she work? What does she do?"

"That's the problem! I still haven't told you that part."

"That's why we're here, so you can tell me", he rested both elbows on the table, staring right at me, still with a slight smile on his face.

"She works at… Knights bar", I enunciated, quietly pronouncing every syllable.

"The bar I took you to that first time?!" His smile erased completely and he put the glasses he'd left on the table back on. Apparently, he wanted to read my body language.

"That same one."

"Who is she? A new waitress? The one who came in to clean the bar? What does she do?" He seemed anxious, his hands restless on the table.

"She's a… she's a stripper."

"What?! Say that again!" he asked very surprised, without taking his eyes off me.

"Yes, she's one of the bar's erotic dancers."

"But, you've already screwed everyone at that place! You told me you were getting married, because you'd already lived everything and that Lisa was the woman of your life. I'd accept what you're telling me from any other man; but, you? You who've played with women as you wanted to, I can't believe it! You know that Lisa is a good woman. That's why you told me you'd leave the bar", he stated, reminding me of the reason why I'd decided to get married, and which I apparently forgot.

"She's new, she arrived on the Friday I told you would be my last night there. I thought about leaving the bar, precisely because of my marriage to Lisa; but... now I don't know. I feel very confused."

"What's the problem, Alex, if you already got what you wanted? Just move away and be done. You know nothing good can come out of that, you know that right?" he stated, staring at me, as if he was trying to bring up a dead issue between us, which we promised we'd never speak about and which I knew hurt him a lot to remember.

"That's the point, brother; I want to, but I can't. It's as if something pushed me to her. Truth is, I don't know what to do John. If you saw her! By God! She's unique, beautiful, a goddess!"

"Do you want some good advice? Just stay away, Alex. You might end up doing something crazy."

We finished our talk and when I got home, after stopping on the way and paying $700 dollars for a new phone, I could only think about the conversation I'd just had with my brother: 'Maybe John's right and I should stay away from her.' 'Maybe I'm still on time'. 'Why did she have to come into my life, right on my last Friday at the bar?' 'What's the reason behind all these?' 'I think it'd be better if I don't return to the bar and just forget all about her'. Days later, I went to the gym.

"How are you, Blondie? What are we doing today?"

"What's wrong with you, Alex? Did you forget it's Monday today?! Arms, as always! Don't tell me it's that girl who's got you like this? Forget about that already! You won't get anywhere with her!" He didn't know about everything that had happened between us.

"Well, for your information, blond Marc... the wolf already hunt its prey", I bragged about my achievement with her; I played the winner.

"No, no, no... I can't believe it! You're the best! Of course, after John!"

"You know that when I set something in mind, I do it, right?" I laughed out loud, wanting to seem a Don Juan. But inside, I knew I was only a child with her.

"Yes, yes, congratulations! But I don't want to hear any more love stories now. Let's do what we came for", he said, tired of hearing about my sexual escapades with women.

After all these came Thursday, Lisa had already planned for us to go to the movies together on Friday. I thought it would be the perfect opportunity to test my feelings and not go to the bar that night. That way, I'd know what I felt for the jet-black skin and mysterious girl, if it was just an obsession of mine, or something more than that.

On Friday, when it was 9:10 pm, Lisa and I went to the movies. We entered the place and I could only think of her... the bar girl and the time at which her show would begin. In as much as I wanted to be there, I couldn't even think about leaving Lisa that night, after what had happened at her sister's birthday.

The movie went on and Lisa and I sat there like the two lovers we were, mere months from getting married. Although my body was with her, my mind was somewhere else. Sometimes, Lisa and I would kiss, eat popcorn and, occasionally, laugh. And although I tried tricking my mind, I couldn't; she was still there. The clock struck 11:20 pm. The movie ended and, apparently, I was about to pass my test of not going to the bar, for the first time in a long time.

I went to Lisa's house; we burned her bedroom sheets with our passion, we were overcome by tiredness and, when I woke up on Saturday morning, I realized that my interruption to my bar visits had been a reality. But the fact that I hadn't gone to see her, didn't mean I hadn't been there, as my mind was with the girl the entire night.

Days went by, and it was Wednesday. Throughout that whole day at the office, I thought of the Friday I didn't go to see her. I wanted to call her and explain why I wasn't able to see her show that night. 'Without her phone number, how could I call her? 'Maybe it's better this way'. 'I need to get her out of my head.' Suddenly, my office door opened.

"Hello, Alex!"

"How are you, John?"

"Remember we need to send the papers to the insurer."

"Sit down, John, I want to tell you something" I requested, asking him to show me the papers he'd brought with him.

"Don't tell me you went out again with the stripper on Friday night?"

"I didn't, but not because I didn't want to, but because I couldn't. I was with Lisa at the movies the whole night; and ended up in her apartment."

"As it should be. What do you have to tell me?"

I stared at my brother and thought about how happy he was with his wife and daughter. Partially, I decided to get married because of him. Since he got married, he never returned to the bar with me. Although, truth is, one could say there was another reason.

"I just haven't been able to stop thinking about her; she's on my mind all the time. I don't know what to do."

"It'd be better if you don't see her anymore, Alex."

"If you saw her, you wouldn't ask that of me."

"Well you'll have to remember that you're getting married in a few months. It doesn't matter how beautiful she is... they're all the same. They're all cut from the same cloth."

"Maybe you're right, brother, and I should stop going to the bar. But, how can I resist the temptation if I have never stopped going for three years straight; last Friday was the first."

"I have the solution... you and I are going out this weekend."

I couldn't believe what my brother had just said. Since he got married, we'd never been to a bar together. He only spent his time getting fat and losing his hair. I think that was one of my fears about marriage. I wouldn't be able to bear getting as fat as he was. At his thirty-seven years, he looked like an old man."

"And you think that will work?"

"I'll be there to make it work, just like old times: wolves in the darkness! Remember? Now I have to go, brother, I have a lot of work", patting me on the back, he left my office, following our agreement.

Truth is I'd never really taken that war cry we used seriously; I even thought I didn't remember it. I believed in his proposal even less; I didn't even remember the last time he and I went together to a bar. At that moment, I thought that following my brother's advice would be best. After all, I owed my first time in the bar to him. I only hoped his strategy would work, to forget about the bar and that bratty girl.

Friday arrived, and my first call of the day was John's, to remind me about our outing that night. With pain in my soul, I told him in insecure words that I hadn't forgotten, that everything was still on. He said he'd pick me up at 8:00 pm. 'Apparently, my brother is serious', 'he's actually coming', I pondered the unthinkable. Hours went by… my watch said 8:13 pm and he hadn't yet arrived. 'I knew it'. 'He's not coming'. 'I thought so', I doubted he'd come. After five minutes, I decided to open my car door, with the firm intention of going to see her. When suddenly…

"Beep… beep…" I heard the car horn twice.

"Hello, John!" When I saw him coming, I noticed it'd be impossible to see her tonight.

"Where do you think you're going, Alex?"

"I thought about looking for you", I pretended to deceive the oldest of wolves.

"Are you sure that's what you wanted to do?! Get in, we're taking my car", he obviously didn't believe me. He knew my tricks well.

"But, we can take both cars, that way you won't have to drive me home", I had a crazy… very crazy idea in mind.

"I'd rather drive you home, than for you to miss where we're going", I knew it wouldn't be easy to evade him to see her that night. Truth is, I was surprised he came.

"Ok" I whispered, with complete resignation.

We went out as planned. We ran for about an hour and a half, I didn't know if it was due to his strategy or why, but he got me as far away from my true intentions as he could.

"Is this the place, John?" at least the front was very elegant. People congregated at the entrance, which meant the place was very busy.

"Yes, Alex. Far away from your lady!" he said smiling, patting me on the shoulder and staring at the front of the establishment.

After passing security, I looked everywhere and found it was very similar to the one I used to go to every Friday; although this wasn't a strip club. My brother even thought about that.

"Do you think this is a good idea, bringing me here to forget her?" He wouldn't stop looking around.

"Have you ever heard about the expression, a nail drives out another!? Perhaps by seeing a different ambiance, you can forget that stripper. And, who knows! Maybe you'll realize it was just a fixation."

We sat there, hours went by and, truth be told, I felt very comfortable with the environment. I didn't think of Alisha much. Time went by and at one point, without knowing why or where she came from… a twenty-something woman came and sat beside me after my brother left me alone to go to the bathroom. I had a slight impression that John knew about that woman's arrival to our table, as the young girl greeted me by name when she sat down; telling me that her name was Tina. I was quite surprised because I'd never been there before. My brother arrived a few minutes later and sat down with us, unsurprised by the woman's presence. Actually, the girl was quite beautiful; blond hair, with a Halle Berry cut; thin, white skin and thin nose; how could I ignore her voluptuous breasts and deep navel, if her little blouse and insinuations allowed me to see me more than I should? She even looked a lot like someone I knew well… my girlfriend Lisa, but younger. It was also too much of a coincidence that she resembled my fiancée. It further confirmed my suspicions that John had something to do with it. As we talked, Tina wouldn't stop flirting with me. I played along, as I could imagine where it was all coming from. She asked me to dance the second time. I told her how bad a dancer I was; however, she insisted, and my brother practically pushed me to dance with her. As they were both so persistent, I agreed to dance with her. Throughout the whole thing, she wouldn't stop insinuating her charms and sensual moves towards me. During the dance, suddenly, she kissed my lips and I got carried away by that kiss. After the song ended and a new one started, I took her hand and led her to our table. Suddenly, I felt pulled backwards... it was her, taking me to one of the bathrooms, closing the door behind us. She kissed me again; this time, I pushed her against one of the walls, passionately responding to her kisses. I dragged her all over the wall, taking her to one of the sinks on which, later, I removed some of her clothes. She, at one point, pulled out a condom, which I didn't even see where she kept. She did it with such agility, she even seemed to have rehearsed it several times. She gave it to me after breaking the wrapper and I agreed to have a quickie with her. I strongly placed her in front of the sink mirror. When I was standing behind her, with my member in her vagina... Alisha came to mind, which made me more aggressive. I spanked her a bit. I squeezed the back of her neck right above her back, looking for the long black hair of the tanned girl I had in mind, and when I saw her face in the mirror we had in front of us, after she raised her chin as I punished her vagina, I knew the one who had her legs spread in front of me with my penis in her was another girl. Although my pleasure was evident, she seemed more relaxed. She bore my sudden movements without complaint. It all ended after a few minutes. The semen filled condom ended up in the trash, and we left the bathroom after having sex. The kind of sex in which only the paying party participates. Her kisses always tasted like purchased kisses. Her vague and emotionless caresses. It was as if she'd changed from one moment to another. She was no longer the girl I met outside the bathroom, the one who fought to get my attention. We both returned to my table. After a few more minutes of conversation, she left. John looked at me and had a very peculiar smile in his face, which said a lot. My watch said 3:23 on Saturday morning. We left and, apparently, the old wolf's masterstroke to keep me away from the stripper had worked. On our way home, he'd look at me from time to time, with the same smile, over and over again. At one point, I asked:

"You sent that girl to the table for me, right?"

"No, why did you say that?" he said erasing his smile, trying to deceive my intelligence.

"Don't play innocent, you know exactly why I'm saying that", he could only see my side as he drove, with his belly almost touching the steering wheel, because of how fat he'd gotten after his wedding.

"Well, yes, I did! But, you liked it, didn't you?" he gave me the same smile.

"Well, to be honest… no! I always thought you'd be behind all that and I confirmed it while we were having sex. Besides her resemblance to Lisa; her kisses and caresses always seemed purchased, like going to the store to get some pants."

"The important thing is that you didn't go to see that stripper that's driving you crazy", he didn't even suspect that, at times, I imagined that the person I was having sex with in that bathroom was her.

"You're right", I smiled, trying to play strong and deceive my true desires.

When I got home, after such a long and hectic day with my brother, I only wanted to sleep. When I woke up that same morning, I noticed that, somehow, John was right. It'd been two Fridays in a row since I'd gone to the bar, unable to see Alisha. I continued my weekly routine:

work, exercises and my desire to forget the young dancer who tormented my life. 'Apparently, my veteran brother was right,' I said to myself that following Thursday. Although I was still thinking of her, my mind's persistence to remember her decreased, I think by as much as fifty percent, which was a lot for me. Days went by, then weeks, since I'd gone for the first time to that distant bar with my brother. I always heard: 'He who's full of tips, dies of old age'; which seemed true, as my older brother's advice was paying off. Everything was going as planned. That doesn't mean I forgot about her completely, but she wasn't so constantly in my mind, hurting me and leaving no room for other thoughts.

## Chapter 5

IT SEEMED incredible that it'd been four months since I met the young stripper at the bar. But the most amazing thing was that I hadn't been back in weeks. I was getting used to not seeing her. I went back to being me. I spent more time with my fiancée and my family. I still thought of her, but not as insistently. I think she was already becoming one more memory. I felt like everything hadn't been more than the adventure I'd seen in her and that now, my girlfriend had gone back to being what we always thought... meant for each other.

It was Friday, and my brother and I went out again. I arrived at my girlfriend's house at the end of the day, at about 2:00 am. The sun came up, my watch said 9:00 on Saturday morning, when my fiancée woke me up. We were getting ready to go shopping. She insisted on accompanying me to buy a gift for my mother, Margaret, who was celebrating her fifty-sixth birthday that day. She accompanied me, knowing that I didn't like going shopping with her. Going shopping with my girlfriend seems boring, and we always lost time, even if she knew what she wanted; but, as this was a present for my mother and they got along very well... too well I'd say —it seemed more like she was her daughter instead of me-, I had no other choice but to accept her company.

So we decided to go in her car to one of the largest shopping centers in New York. We spent hours unable to find the perfect gift for my mother, as I'd anticipated. At one point, I decided to separate from Lisa for a few minutes, while she saw something she liked. We separated on the 9th floor. I took the elevator to go to the fast food area, located on the first floor. I needed something because the hangover I'd gotten from drinks with my brother the night before was killing me. I needed water, it was urgent. When my girlfriend called me, telling me she'd finally found something for my mother and asking me to go back upstairs to see it, I went back to the elevator. In it, there was only a fat and ugly lady, who didn't stop talking from the moment I stepped in.

"What floor are you going to young man?"

"9th floor please", I rested my back on one of the cold metal walls. It helped cool down my body.

"I don't trust these elevators. If it weren't for all these shopping bags I'm carrying I'd take the stairs", she murmured relentlessly.

'I really just want to drink my water in calmness, lady, shut up!' 'My God, this woman talks too much!'

"These elevators scare me, sir. Don't they scare you?"

'Take the stairs, then.' 'I'd love to see her go upstairs with all that fat'. I nodded in answer, that way, I wouldn't engage in a conversation with her. In that metal box, my only priority was my water bottle.

"Can you imagine, sir, if this elevator stopped halfway? My God, no! Deliver us from that!"

'But, by God, where's this lady's off button?' 'I prefer the stairs to this woman, my God.' 'I don't know what's worse, my discomfort or her'. When we stopped on the 4th floor, as this was her stop, I raised my head and lifted my right elbow to have a sip of water. 'Cheers'. 'Finally, I'll get rid of her'. 'Get out quickly I'm in a hurry'. My mind was celebrating the lady's arrival at her destination. The elevator opened and while the fat ugly lady with a talkative parrot complex got out, another person was waiting to make her entrance... her dress was light pink, very elegant and ruffled on the knees, (nothing like the old, fat, ugly lady getting out), with a belt of a slightly darker shade of the same color; thin high-heeled shoes, also pink, matching her belt and satchel; pink lipstick which apparently matched her dress on purpose; her hair was black, all gathered up in a bun held by a butterfly-shaped clip, dark skin and with a very sensual walk. Surprise! I was seeing her and couldn't believe it... Alisha herself was walking into the elevator. I think she only took about four steps, but I counted about ten. Those were the longest steps I'd seen in my life. At that moment, I couldn't talk. The sip of water got stuck in my throat like strong lemon juice. I must've coughed a couple of times, swallowing my lemon juice... sorry, right, it was water! I wasn't thinking clearly. I asked myself if I was asleep and still dreaming. Until I heard her voice say...

"Hello, Alex!" It was at that moment I realized it was all really happening. It wasn't an illusion.

"How are you, Alisha?" I greeted her when I caught back my breath and after assimilating her presence, so close to me. I finished my water in seconds. The plastic bottle in my hand made an irritating noise, due to the squeezes it was giving it with my fingers, driven by nerves.

"Well, you see, shopping. And what are you looking for?" I could also see she was surprised to see me.

"Buying something I need", I didn't want to go into details, since I was with my girlfriend and didn't want her to know.

As we talked, the elevator kept going up, indicating the increasing numbers in red. The moment came in which, suddenly, it stopped between the 5th and 6th floor, without reaching the door, which meant we were both alone and locked in those four walls. 'Wow the old lady was right'. 'She spoke so much of the elevator and of the chances of it breaking down, that it did', I thought in my nervousness.

At that moment, I panicked a little and looked at the young girl, to see if she was in the same situation as me. However, she seemed calm, something which seemed irregular in a woman, given the circumstances. Unexpectedly, I noticed her index finger on my lips, caressing me softly. My heart began to beat faster, when she pushed her body onto mine.

"Would you dare…?" She whispered, placing her lips on my right ear and decreasing the space between her arms and the wall where my back was resting.

"What do you mean?" I played innocent, not because I wanted to, but because of how nervous she made me.

"Shall I explain it and waste time? Or will you make up your mind and we both win?" She whispered, removing the butterfly from her hair, dropping her hair in a single blow onto her shoulders and back.

"But… we're in a public place, Alisha!" I was very nervous and surprised by what she was asking.

"We're in an elevator, Alex" she stated softly, throwing her hair forward. She was flirting with my weakness.

"But, somebody could come and find us", I accepted every kiss and caress she gave me, despite my nerves and the panic I felt.

"Then, Alex…?" She looked into my eyes, biting her lower lip and placing paused kisses on my neck.

"I do! But… I don't know, somebody could come", I was dying to make love to her, to kiss her lips, kiss all of her, but it didn't seem like the most appropriate place. Besides, I thought of Lisa and, above all, I was afraid of not knowing what would happen with the elevator and its breakdown.

"Well, then… you better start… now!

Right then, she put her finger on my mouth. This time, silencing me, imprisoning all my cheap excuses and fears. Hot blood ran through my veins, forcing me to take her waist strongly and imprison her body to mine. I kissed her lips passionately and crazily, completely forgetting my panic. She responded by biting mine, sometimes, staying on my lower lip and mine on hers. She squeezed my neck tightly, with her left leg, as I pulled up her dress, caressing one of her legs; taking it to my hips and squeezing her buttocks with my fingers, making up for lost time. I started playing inside of her panties with one of my hands, and I managed to touch her vagina with my fingers, feeling how wet it was. She sighed with pleasure dropping her purse on the floor, as we had sex against the clock. Knowing that at any moment they'd come to inspect why the elevator had stopped, excited us even more. This time, there was no condom between her sex and mine. I carried her from one wall to another, stumbling around, cornering her in one of the four corners of that metal box. I took out one of her breasts in whichever way I could, gently biting her nipple. She pressed my head to her bosom even more, asking me to bite it again; she stroked my hair and screamed my name endlessly. In the comings and goings of our sexes, our moans echoed in those four walls. She noticed some very thin silver tubes on the elevator, at our waist height, possibly placed there to place one's hands. Apparently her weakness and agility with them prompted her to raise one of her legs on one of the tubes, giving me a better view of her vagina, which gave me more space to move my body more easily. She looked into my eyes, when she no longer had any strength to keep going. It was obvious what she was asking for with that look. We were already defeated by pleasure... when we heard noises outside the elevator. The elevator went up to the 6th floor, fully opening its doors... and there we were, standing inside, far away from each other. She begged the technicians for forgiveness, explaining that pushing the emergency button had been a mistake. And even though they could assume what had happened, they simply did their inspection work. Once they let us use the same elevator, one of them said:

"Your collar… sir! You might want to fix it; it's a bit out of place."

'When are they going to put mirrors in the elevators?' We continued to where we were going, up from the 6th floor. We were smiling, after acting as we did nothing in the metal box, and fixing our clothing.

"I can't believe you made me do something like that, Alisha? How could you push that button?" I couldn't get rid of the tiny smile I had on my face, and I loved hers; she had a half-smile, but it was very cute and playful.

"Oh! Now I made you do it? You could've said no when I asked", I loved how she said things, when she wanted to be funny.

"I would've never had the courage to do that if you didn't make me. At least, you could've told me about the button. You're amazing, Alisha!" I could not avoid showing my satisfaction with what had happened, despite the panic I felt at first.

"Do you really think so, Alex?! Well that's me, very determined" she whispered, kissing my cheek.

"Why are you like this with me, Alisha? There's something that puzzles me. Why did you pick me that night, among all those businessmen? Why did you give me that direct look, when it was others who were placing money on your body? What do you want of me, besides driving me crazy with your follies and mysteries...?" I wanted answers for my fears and concerns.

"I've told you not to ask so many questions. There'll come a day in which you may ask the wrong question and the answer could change what we have..." I didn't expect that answer. Her way of treating me was confusing; the way in which she evaded my questions.

"I don't know, your mysteries confuse me. I just want to clarify so many things in me, but you don't let me", I looked into her eyes, looking for something that would tell me what that woman was hiding.

"Please, don't make me lose you right now, Alex..."

At that moment, without us noticing, the elevator doors opened on the ninth floor. I couldn't believe who was standing outside the elevator, about to enter… my fiancée. She looked inside the elevator and realized I was talking to the girl.

"But, Alex! What the hell happened to you? Didn't you say you'd come up half an hour ago?" she yelled ominously, with her white skin turning redder than the dress she was wearing. Not to mention how surprised she was to see how we were talking.

"Lisa, sorry... what happened was that, while… when we were going up with another lady, when we got to the sixth floor, the elevator stopped and a few minutes later they came to correct the damage. So we couldn't come up until now", I answered nervously and with my heart pounding.

"I was coming to get you, Alex! And what do you mean 'we'?! Who is she?! Why were you having such an enjoyable conversation?" her jealousy, upon seeing such a beautiful girl at my side, was as evident as her anger. Watching us, she wouldn't let go of the elevator door, preventing them from closing.

"My name is Alisha..."

Before she could say anything else, I played a card that for better or worse changed the whole picture.

"This is Alisha! Remember the young girl I told you about? The one I ran over with my car the night of your sister, Luisa's birthday, remember?" After making up such a thing, I thought on how daring I was, involving the girl in my easy way out.

"Yes, I remember. But what does that have to do with all of this?" Her anger was still evident, as her blue eyes shone more brightly when she was angry.

"Well, this is her... she's the girl!" I said, risking everything, without knowing what the girl's reaction would be. At that moment, I thought my entire world would collapse. I could only see the girl's surprised face, upon hearing what I was making up to muddle through. I could see beyond the glow that emanated from her eyes. Her face, rather than surprised, seemed pained. I didn't think what I said would affect her so much. My girlfriend and I were still talking and she seemed not to be there. It was as if she'd immersed herself in memories, as if she was in another world.

"Oh, this is the girl!" She scanned her entire body from top to bottom, with burning eyes and flushed cheeks.

"Yes, she is. This is Alisha" I could only see the girl's face and in my mind, I imagined the questions that were going through her head. That surprised expression on her face worried me. It was as if she was wondering... what's going on here?

"Hello, Lisa. I'm Alisha; after the accident, now Alex's friend", she introduced herself sarcastically, after returning the real world.

"Nice to meet you! I'm Lisa, Alex's fiancée" with that greeting, she clearly wanted to state who she was and what role she played in my life.

"Ah! You're his fiancée?" she kept using sarcasm in each of her answers.

I was breathing slowly, as someone getting honey serum, since that moment had become eternal for me.

At one point, I said goodbye to the young girl, leaving the elevator, leaving her behind and trying to get my girlfriend as far away from that dangerous encounter as I could. Lisa, still in shock, wouldn't let go of the elevator door. Something that was still worrying me.

"Where are you headed, Alisha?" my tension increased with Lisa's questions to the girl.

"After buying the thing I have to get from the tenth floor, I'll be done with my shopping and then, I'd be on my way home."

"Why don't you give me a few minutes of your time and come with Alex and me? I'd like to know your opinion on something I'm showing my fiancé for his mother; it's a birthday gift."

'My God! Lisa, let's go now!'. Without allowing the girl to answer her question, I said:

"Love, let's go, she has to get something from the tenth floor, she already said so. Then she needs to go home. I imagine! Whatever you pick is fine. Don't worry so much about it", I was trying to get my girlfriend away from the elevator to be able to breathe more easily.

I only wanted the minutes to end. To my surprise, they were just getting started. I noticed that when I let go of my girlfriend's hand which was preventing the elevator door from closing, she asked the girl. But... before the elevator closed, Alisha placed her left foot between the two doors.

"Thinking about it...! It's not a bad idea! I'll come with you", she looked at me with those amazed and questioning eyes. She seemed uncomfortable with my attitude.

From that moment, they both walked towards the store, as if they'd known each other their whole lives. I walked behind them, listening to every word of their conversation.

"How are you after the accident, Alisha?" each of my girlfriend's questions were like a stab to my body.

"Well, much better; as you can see, it wasn't so serious."

"You're very beautiful. Do you have a boyfriend, Alisha?"

"I don't."

"How can a girl so beautiful and elegant as you not have a boyfriend?" even I was dying to hear that answer. It was a question I'd always wanted to ask.

"I don't believe in men and their lies... no offense to your boyfriend", she answered, turning to see me, and with the same sarcasm she'd used before.

Their conversation was making me more and more nervous. I asked God that we could choose the gift as soon as possible and get out of there.

We finally got to the store and my girlfriend showed the girl a $ 10,000 French ceramic vase, for my mother. Without even thinking twice, I nodded, accepting her proposal.

"What do you think, Alisha?"

"Can I really say what I think or should I just say what you want to hear?"

"I hope you can tell me what you think", said Lisa.

"Truth is, I don't like it at all… I think it's a gift she'll see like yet another ornament, on her way from the living room to the kitchen", her answer didn't surprise me. Since she held the vase, I noticed she didn't like it.

"It's just that we've searched all morning and we still don't have a gift for my mother-in-law, Margaret."

'By God, Lisa! Just take the blessed vase and let's go, damn it!' 'Forget about her opinion.' 'What does she know', screamed my head which was about to burst.

"Yes, I imagine how difficult it must be to give something to someone who has it all", she masked her sarcasm with a smile.

"But then, what are we giving your mother, Alex?"

"I say we should take it. I like it and I know my mother will love it", I wanted to end the tension, no matter what that spoilt child thought.

"If you allow me, may I suggest something?" asked the girl, giving Lisa a sideway glance.

'No more, Alisha, please!'. 'Just let us take that vase.' 'This is why I can't stand shopping with women.' 'It's a waste of time', I kept on thinking about how complicated the situation was.

"Of course you can, Alisha!" answered my girlfriend, giving another stab to my despair.

"I think you've only been concentrating on how expensive it is and not in what you really want to give her. If you'd like, we can go to the tenth floor, where I have to make my last purchase and pick something for her, perhaps it won't be as expensive! But that doesn't mean it won't be valuable."

"Maybe you're right. What do you think, Alex?"

"Ah...? Yes, Lisa. I think she's right."

In the whole gift process, only I was at a loss, as I was still at an edge, because even though we'd spent half a day shopping, we were still as before... empty-handed.

'Who knew I'd be with these two women in one place, looking for a gift for my mother?'. 'When I tell this to John, he won't believe me.'

We got to the tenth floor, after the three of us boarded the elevator together, as if we'd known each other for years.

"Alisha, that's a book store!" said my girlfriend, very surprised.

"Yes, it is, Lisa."

Right at that moment, I thought about the book I'd seen in her apartment, the same time she tied me to her shower.

"But, I can't imagine Alex and me arriving with a book as a present for his mother. How could that be?"

"Remember, that the only thing you can give to a person who has everything in life… is knowledge", she answered, searching among the shelves and giving some titles to my fiancée.

'Right, knowledge.' 'Of course!' 'The same knowledge you acquired with those erotic books you have in your apartment's living room'. 'I just hope you don't recommend those books to my girlfriend.' 'Remember that my mother is turning fifty-six years', shouted my mind.

"You're right, Alisha. Apart from being very beautiful and young, you're very smart. At my thirty-five, I would've never thought of something like that."

"Thank you, Lisa! You're also very cute. Look at this children's book, Amelia – looking for the cure; it's beautiful for a mother! or this one, Life's fair; or this, Life Lesson. I've read them all and they're very good; but if I can recommend one, I'd say buy this one, Enjoy everything you have, even if it may seem little, it's served me well.

'Please, Alisha, enough is enough! Just give her anything'. 'Just don't give her anything erotic, I don't want my mother chaining my old man', I thought desperately, crazy to escape that bad dream.

"Ok, we'll take that one. I'll trust your taste", she said, taking the book from her hands and walking to the registry.

After that choice, I just wanted to pay and leave; I couldn't take the pressure anymore. I wanted to separate the two women that were confusing my existence at that moment. Shopping was over.

'Now I can breathe easily,' I said to myself, as we all took the elevator down, as if joined by an old friendship. They continued talking like good friends, laughing loudly; instead, my seriousness was tomb-like. I was counting the red numbers down, like in a countdown. When we reached the first floor, we walked to the exit.

"Bye, Alisha!" I extended my hand and got into my girlfriend's car.

"Bye, Alex."

But my girlfriend asked a question that would complicate everything. And then something I never expected happened...

"And your car, Alisha?"

"I don't have a car."

"How are you leaving?" Asked my girlfriend, very surprised that there could be a woman without a car in the world.

'Jeez, Lisa, let's go!' 'There are thousands of taxis and trains In New York'. 'How do you think she got here?'

"I'll take a taxi. Don't worry."

"No, Alisha. Let us take you home."

When I heard my girlfriend propose such a thing to the girl, I was stunned. I couldn't believe Lisa had said that.

"No, Lisa. Thank you very much", hearing her refusal gave me the relief I sought. But... my torment was just beginning.

"I have a better idea, girl... since it was you who chose my future mother-in-law's present, I'd like you to come with us to the family reunion; we'll have to celebrate it."

'What are you saying?' 'What are you thinking?' 'My girlfriend has gone mad!' 'What do you mean to the party!'. 'This was the only thing missing', I was burning inside. Before Alisha could answer:

"Come on, Lisa, we'll be late. She must be tired", I think this was what further complicated the situation. Even though she's already said she didn't want to get in the car, she looked at me with eyes that said: 'You don't decide for me'. Then she opened her mouth to say:

"Very well, Lisa. I accept, I'll go with you", my shoulders slumped like Jell-O. 'Make me vanish right now', I thought upon hearing her.

She got in the car with us and our trip to my parents' house began when the clock struck 1:23 pm. Truth is, I didn't understand why she had accepted that invitation to my parents' house. It was as if she wanted to get back at me, for having gotten her into that mess. In her face I could see she was enjoying my anguish. And I couldn't say anything; I could only let the current take me away.

# *Chapter 6*

**WE ARRIVED** at my parents' house. My girlfriend and Alisha walked in front of me with my mother's present. I decided to make sure that the conversation didn't divert, in case the girl ended up telling her everything. Due to how little I knew her, I could tell that she was impulsive and direct. Upon entering, my girlfriend began to introduce the girl as our friend. Alisha seemed to be more of her friend than mine.

"This is Mrs. Margaret and he is Mr. Frank, Alex's parents. They're practically my parents too", stated Lisa, with a splendid smile on her lips.

"Nice to meet you, ma'am; and you too, Mr. Frank. I wish you happiness on this day and in the days ahead, Mrs. Margaret", she said, politely extending a hand to my parents with a gorgeous smile.

"So nice to meet you too. She's a very educated and beautiful girl. Come, come Lisa. We're all gathered in the garden, we're only waiting for my son, John, and his wife, Marian, and their daughter, Lina. Wait until you meet her, Alisha. She's a lovely girl, a darling! Apparently my son, Alex will be the next one to give me a grandchild. If you could see how much he struggled with his decision to get married...!" said my mother, with the glamor that characterized her, extending her hand to the girl and telling her the whole story on the way to the garden.

I, in the meantime, kept out of everything that was happening, but very aware of what was being said. Introductions were just starting. We went to the garden, where they kept on introducing her to our closest family friends. Among them was my sister Sara. A really good chemistry sparked between them; perhaps because they were of a similar age, as my sister was twenty-four.

Later, I had to get away from them, as they were gossiping... sorry, having a women's meeting and none of them wanted me to come close. After thirty-five minutes or so, the person that really worried me arrived... my brother, John, with his wife and daughter, Lina. After greeting him, I wanted to introduce the girl to my brother:

"I can't see Lisa or Alisha anywhere! Where are they?" I asked my sister Sara, when I lost sight of them.

"Lisa is taking Alisha to the bathroom", she said, worrying me with her answer.

"Why didn't you take her, Sara?" my concern was noticeable.

"Why does it matter if it was me or her who took her?"

"Because, well you're the one who lives with our parents and knows the house better."

"Alex, what's wrong with you? Why are you acting this way? I know you better than anyone. Something's up, brother. Don't tell me you like that girl? You can't fool me!"

"No way, Sara! She's a friend to both of us", I was trying to get that idea out of her head.

"I know that, brother! I'm just playing with you. I don't think you could do that to your girlfriend, you two are about to get married. Remember you're not that kid who jumped from girl to girl anymore, without measuring the consequences, you're getting married!"

In the end, I had to get away from her, so I wouldn't tell her what she already suspected. John continued greeting the guests. However, I kept on thinking about the two women who were confusing my existence. 'Where are they?' 'I just hope Alisha didn't end up telling what happened to my girlfriend.' 'Together, they're a danger to me.' 'Pure dynamite', I was mortified by what could happen. Then, my brother and I moved away from the crowd. We sat on a bench of the many located around the lawn, facing the house door. My intention at that moment, being all alone, was to tell him what was happening, because since he'd arrived, he hadn't seen her. When I was about to tell him everything, right at the moment in which I was getting the words out of my mouth… crossing the door, there were Lisa and Alisha. We were about 25 or 30 feet away from them. John, upon seeing the long hair elegant woman walking upright:

"Brother, who's that beautiful girl walking with your girlfriend? I hadn't seen that friend of Lisa's before! Who in the world can be the owner of such a hottie?!" he asked, very impressed by the girl's beauty.

"That's Alisha", I muttered under my breath.

"I know that's Lisa. I mean the girl walking with her, the one with dark long hair", he stated, confusing my answer.

"That's who I'm talking about. I said… Alisha, not Lisa."

"And who's Alisha?" he asked, with a mischievous smile on his face.

"It's the young girl I've been talking so much about… the stripper."

"The stripper from the bar?! The one you're screwing?" he asked surprised, completely erasing the smile from his face.

"That's her! The same one."

"But, have you gone mad Alex?! What the hell is she doing here? Why did you bring her? What were you thinking?" He yelled with his teeth clenched, but with noticeable anger.

"That's the thing, brother; I didn't bring her. Lisa brought her."

"Now, I really don't understand anything. Can you explain this, please?" he stood up from the bench and faced me.

"I'll tell you everything; but sit, so you want fall."

When I told him what had happened, he couldn't believe it; although I didn't tell him what had happened in the elevator. He was stunned at the story I had just told him.

While I was with my brother, trying to find a solution to the problem, Lisa and the others called us to open some presents. We arrived at the table where all the gifts were, surrounded by the crowd. I realized Alisha had already become a sensation among those present. At that moment, she was playing with Lina's long hair, who was comfortably standing next to her. John called his daughter to go to his arms, in a rather blatant way. This actually bothered me quite a bit.

After my mother had opened a few presents, it was the time to open ours; among all of them, it was the smallest one. My mother tore the wrapping paper and, upon seeing the book, was stunned, and everyone present silently wondered why Lisa and I had given that tiny trinket to my mother. But to everyone's surprise, upon seeing the title and the book cover, she pounced on my fiancée, thanking her for such a nice present. Undoubtedly, she assumed it hadn't been my idea to buy it. To be honest, I never had faith in that gift. I simply accepted that my girlfriend was going to buy it for the sake of it. I always thought about buying another one, as expensive or more than the ones she'd already opened, on our way to my parents' house; but given that Alisha was coming with us, I dismissed the idea. My girlfriend, Lisa, was very generous and after such a warm hug, she told my mother that she actually had to thank the girl, as it'd been her who'd suggested and chosen her gift. I'd always seen my mother read one book or another, but I never thought she'd get so excited over a cheap book. My brother, upon hearing that the girl had been the one who'd chosen our mother's gift, gave me a puzzled look. Taking me to a place far from the crowd, he told me:

81

"Alex, how could you allow that nobody to choose a trinket for our mother?" He expressed angrily.

"But mother loved the book, what's the problem?"

"God knows how much you paid for such an ordinary gift! How much did you pay for that stupid book?" he asked very upset.

"$17.99", I answered his stupid question, wanting to turn around and head back to the crowd.

"How could you accept something like that? That woman is making you lose the notion of who you are and what she is", he said, stopping me and belittling the girl.

"But, tell me, John, how many of the presents opened before and after did my mother like as much as the book? Neither the one that cost $10,000 nor the one that cost $2,200, not even yours. She enjoyed the $17.99 one more. Doesn't that tell you anything?" I answered, turning back to him.

"Alex, can't you notice that the prostitute is already getting not only into your life, but also in our, your family?" his anger was evident, with both the girl and with me. He couldn't stand her being there. I think he was speaking more due to his memories of that bar, than of what has actually happening.

"Why do you call her like that, John?" I couldn't stand the attitude he had towards the girl, which is why my voice also raised, reaching a higher note.

"How do you want me to call her? Have you forgotten where she works, what she does there... I have to remind you that she dances naked!"

"She doesn't dance naked and you know it. Remember that it's a topless bar."

"It's the same, Alex, the same; they're all the same, you need to take her out of here now! I don't know how you'll do it, because I could… I think I could… tell everyone who she is and what she really does", he stated, giving me an ultimatum.

"Why do you act like that with her, you don't even know her, John?" our discussion was becoming increasingly heated.

"You know better than anyone that I know them all, don't you realize she's a gold digger! Look at how happy she is, winning over our family and guests, God knows, to ask them for what. And ask God that she never touches my daughter again, because I don't know what I'd do!"

"I'm not going to let you offend her in such a way. You don't know her, to have that concept of her", my defense was getting him even angrier. It irritated him to see her smile in the crowd. It was as if that fueled his anger.

What began as explanations had become a discussion among brothers. John left, leaving me with the warning of taking the girl away from the celebration. I went to where the guests were, grabbed Alisha's arm, with great delicacy and discretion, and asked her if she wanted me to take her home. Right at that moment, Sara came.

"Come on, Alisha, this is just starting!" she yelled, very excited, grabbing her arm and pulling her body with determination.

"No, sis, I'm taking her home", I couldn't allow her to take her back to the party.

83

"But, why do you want to leave, Alisha? It's still early."

"Yes, I have stuff to do at home; I only came for a bit because Lisa insisted I should accompany her. Could you say goodbye to her and the others for me, please?" she explained, smiling at Sara and kissing her on the cheek.

"Sis, can I borrow your car to take her? Tell Lisa I took her, please."

"Ok, Alex. Remember to visit us one day, Alisha. I like you very much!"

I decided to take the girl to her house; she simply remained quiet the entire way, as if she was expecting me to explain something about what was happening and why she was suddenly involved in all that.

"Alisha, I'm sorry I didn't tell you I had a girlfriend and for getting you out of my parents' house like that" I was trying to break the ice between us and explain my attitude.

"One, you don't have to apologize for having a girlfriend, because I don't care if you do or don't; two, you didn't get me out of there, I decided to leave because I know myself well and I don't know why, but suddenly, your brother started looking at me in a very uncomfortable way."

"Don't worry about John, I have to discuss this with him very seriously."

"Alex, I want you to know, and make it clear, I don't see what has happened between us beyond what it's been. I want to know, why did you use me for your lies? What was that about crashing your car one night? I still don't understand anything. After that, I don't need any more explanations about your family or your fiancée or anyone else."

"Let me explain why I did it... I had no choice and I couldn't think of anything else."

"Well, I hope you never use me for your follies again, please I beg of you."

As much as I explained it all to her, she didn't like that mess at all; especially the thing about the alleged accident. Apparently, that was what bothered her the most. We arrived at her house and she got out of the car, without even waiting for me, as a gentleman, to open her door. She walked and I followed her footsteps, but when we reached the door and when I had expected to go in with her:

"This is where you stay", she said, turning towards me and placing a hand on my chest.

"But, I explained everything", I was trying to get a pass to her house, due to my intense desire to be with her.

"It's not about that. I told you, I don't care for explanations, Alex. You already had your dose of sex for today; so for now, there's nothing else to do, goodbye!"

"But, why, Alisha?" I yelled, trying to get into her apartment again.

"When are you going to learn not to ask questions? I told you, the day will come when you will ask the wrong one, and that question could change what we have... goodbye, Alex."

Then, she closed the door, without giving me a chance to fix the whole misunderstanding. I had to get back to the party and explain to everyone why the young charismatic girl, who'd conquered everyone at the party, had to leave. They didn't understand the way in which she'd left the party. That was something that only my brother and I knew about. Convincing my sister, Sara, and Lisa about Alisha's departure was the hardest thing; as, according to them, in such a short time, they'd had very good chemistry. I looked for John, to discuss his attitude with the girl. I found him in the garden. I called him aside and began the conversation.

"Brother, I need to talk to you", I said, discreetly, taking his arm.

"I know what you want to talk about, Alex."

"Why did you behave like that towards Alisha? I didn't like your attitude, John."

"Don't you see what you're getting into? She's just like..."

"Hello boys, what are you looking for, all alone over here?" asked Lisa, taking us by surprise.

"Nothing, honey", I answered, when I saw her standing in front of us.

"Why those faces? What's happening? Were you fighting...?"

"No, honey, how do you think? We were talking about the factory, right John...?"

"Yes, Lisa, you know... work things", for a moment I thought he'd tell everything to my fiancée, based on the look he gave me.

"Are you sure it was about that? It looked like something else", apparently, she wasn't quite convinced.

"Come on, love, it's nothing. Bye, brother, we'll talk at the office", I had to end the conversation and take Lisa with me. I thought it'd be best, before my brother thought of mentioning anything else.

After everything was calmer and after some time, Lisa and I went to her apartment. I was trying to forget everything that had happened with Alisha, but it seemed impossible because Lisa reminded me, at all times, about how much she'd liked her. She listed each of her virtues; she was so smart, friendly, pretty, etc., without suspecting who she was in my life. She talked so much about the girl, we ended up having sex.

Days went by. Wednesday arrived and my relationship with my brother was no longer the same. We couldn't talk without the name, Alisha, emerging in every conversation. He insisted that I needed to forget about her. Friday was coming, and to tell the truth, I didn't know whether I'd be able to resist the temptation of going to the bar and seeing her again. I didn't know how she'd behave, after what had happened, after having practically closed the door against my face that day.

'I don't know what her plans are, for me, now'. 'I'm dying to see her again'. 'She's dug into my soul like an obsession', I couldn't stop thinking about her. It was as if I didn't want to see her away from me for a second. I wasn't sure if it was love, obsession or a simple whim; but I felt like I wanted to have her always with me, just as she was in my mind.

Sometimes, I thought of what could happen if Lisa found out about everything and how she'd react. To be honest, I no longer knew if it was Lisa or Alisha, for whom I sighed and breathed every day. 'My family would never accept my relationship with her' 'What would happen if they actually knew who she was, or what she does for a living?' 'I wonder if Alisha really feels something for me'. 'Or if I'm just another one in her list, which I imagine must be very long, due to what she does'. 'Maybe I'm getting all excited about her love and she just sees me as a plaything.' 'But how can I find out, without risking my feelings?' 'This is killing me!' These were the questions tormenting my mind and heart.

Friday came and my relationship with John was the same or worse than before. Since the day we argued about her, nothing was well between us; which is why, that day, we didn't even plan to continue our strategy to forget her. The situation was helpless.

I decided to return to the bar. This time, rather than just seeing her, I needed some answers to my many questions and concerns. I sat at my table and after my third drink, that night, she came on, and to my surprise... nothing had changed in the way she acted. How she danced around the pole, her way of looking at me, her sensuality, her persistence on me, were all the same. To be honest, I was expecting a different type of reaction from her, due to what had happened. At the end of her show, as always, she disappeared with a few steps. I waited for her at the parking lot, as I often did when she was done. This time, I had to talk with her friend for a bit, who was waiting for her to drive her home like every night.

"How are you, Rosa?" I said when I saw her friend, the redhead.

"Good, Alex."

"If you want, you can go, I'll take her home tonight" I was looking for a chance to be alone with Alisha.

"I'm sorry, Alex, but she has to decide that. If she asks me to go when she comes out, I will", she said, with the strong attitude that always characterized her, shaking her red hair.

"I understand, can I ask you a question, Rosa?"

"Sure, Alex."

"Have you known Alisha for long?" I said, trying to find out more about the woman who interrupted my dreams.

"Yes, actually, it was I who got her a job here", she answered still playing with her hair.

"Has she always been like this? So mysterious! Why is she determined to play with me? She does it as if I was one of the many men I imagine she has", I said, very confused by what I was feeling, and jealous of the men who enjoyed her show every Friday.

"Look, Alex, don't get me wrong, but she is as she is. If you want answers to your questions, you'll have to ask her and not me. I'm not the best person for you to talk to about her in this way. What I can tell you is that she's the best person I've met in my life. And although, you may have a different concept of my friend, I'm not one to tell you if you're wrong or not. The one I have for her is the best I've ever had of anyone. And I can add: next time, watch your words when you speak about her in front of me. She's been and will always be like a sister to me", she said, leaving her hair and standing in front of me, with a scarily defensive attitude.

"I'm sorry, Rosa, but this is killing me. Her mysteries, her attitude changes. The live-in-the-day attitude she has, without caring or bothering about anything, confuses me."

"I already told you, Alex, only she can answer that. It's time for you to find out for yourself. There she is, look!" she said, pointing and looking over my shoulder.

I turned my head to look back. Indeed, there she came into the parking lot, like a goddess. 'Whoever saw her after the show would've never guessed she was the same person who danced on that blessed pole every Friday.' 'She dresses so differently, elegant, yet, sexy'. 'I've never seen another woman walk that way'. 'My God, she looks beautiful!'

"Hello, Alex", she said, arriving at my side, kissing me on the cheek.

"How are you, Alisha?"

"What are you doing here?" she asked, surprised to see me.

"I want to talk to you. Please!"

"Alis, should I wait for you or are you going with Alex?" asked her redhead friend with a lawyer complex.

"It's ok, Rosa, you can go. Of course...! If Alex decides to take me", she looked at me with sweetness and irony.

"You can go, Rosa. I'll take her home", I couldn't believe she wasn't mad at me. She looked calm. What's more! She looked much more accommodating than in previous times.

'Why does she live this way?' 'I'd love to understand her way of living life.' 'She acts as if nothing had happened'. 'I just hope Rosa won't tell her everything I said'.

"I'll see you later, Rosa", she said goodbye, kissing her on the cheek.

"So, Alex, are we talking here or are you taking me somewhere else?" Very gently, she ran her left hand through my hair. It was like she'd just lit the candle. I melted every time she touched me.

"Where would you like to go?"

"Let's go to your car and we'll see", she said calmly.

We headed to my car and started driving around aimlessly, as neither of us knew where we would end up. At least, that's what I thought… until she began guiding me, as always. After driving for a while and after a few vague words in the car, we ended up at a beach, whose name I didn't even know.

"I want us to finish the night here, Alex", she said softly, stroking the hair behind my neck with her fingers.

"Of course, Alisha. As you say", her amazingly peaceful attitude didn't cease to amaze me, despite all the hype I'd caused. "Why do you want that, Alisha?" I had no idea of what we were there for, in such a dark moment and in a secluded beach.

"When will you learn not to ask questions? But for your peace of mind, we're not here by chance. I wanted you to take me to see the sea and the moonlight, to walk along the sand with you", her plan seemed rather romantic.

"But, it's late for a walk in the beach, don't you think?"

"Why are you always so afraid of everything and everyone?" she asked, giving me a soft look, a look I hadn't seen in her.

"Alisha, I want to apologize for not telling you about my girlfriend and for what happened that day. I'm not sure if you forgave or not. This feeling is killing me! It's like I can't get you out of my head; I tried a thousand times, and I can't just do it."

"I've already told you there's nothing to forgive. I don't care if you have a girlfriend or not. I've never asked for any explanation and I never will... Alex, can I ask of you?" she changed the subject, undeterred. She took my hand and we walked together.

"Whatever you want. I don't think there's anything in this world I wouldn't give you", I don't know why I felt so weak in her presence. She could've asked for the moon, and I think, somehow, that night I would've brought it down for her.

"Promise me that before marrying your fiancée, you won't stop seeing me" she said, making me stop and looking into my eyes.

Her eyes that night had a different glow. She didn't have the impressive look she always gave me, nor that commanding expression in her words.

"Stop seeing you? I couldn't, even if you hadn't asked", I answered, taking her hands and kissing her lips.

"But, promise me! If you want, you can also refuse and I swear nothing will change between us. I swear!"

she said, her eyes teary and holding my hands, inviting me to sit on the sand with her.

I didn't understand that sudden change in her. She seemed like a different person. I never imagined seeing her like that.

"I promise I will, Alisha", I swore, stroking her cheeks and kissing her again.

"I would also like you to make a dream of mine true tonight… it was my intention to come here with you."

"And what's your wish?" I was willing to do anything; even tying me to a tree and doing whatever she wanted to me.

"Tonight, I want to walk along the beach with you. It has always been a dream of mine, walking at night along sand, with someone special, and dip our feet in, holding hands."

"That's your dream? So simple?" I asked, like a stupid guy, thinking it was a bit cheesy for me. Disregarding the fact that she thought I was someone special in her life.

"It may seem simple for you: but for me, it's a dream. Now, let's just walk, Alex. I don't want the moon to disappear, before I can fulfill one of my greatest desires," she said, taking my hand, we both got up from the sand. I was shaking the sand off my pants while she just wanted to run with me.

I couldn't understand how that strong and uniquely temperamental woman had changed so radically from one moment to another. It was as if she was covered with some kind of shell, and upon seeing the moon, it had suddenly fallen on the sand. Right at that moment, an Alisha I'd never seen before appeared. I never thought I'd see something like that in her; it completely disarmed me. I remember she took my arm and we ran along the shore, wetting our feet and clothes, like two lovers. I confess that, at times, I felt cheesy, as if that sort of scene wasn't really for me; as if such ridiculousness didn't fit in my world. I saw her settling her head on my shoulder, and when she did, she confused mine even more, because instead of reclaiming my actions, and wrapping her name in my lies, it was relaxed and giving me a night I didn't expect. The weakness she was showing me, confused my feelings.

After our run along the beach, we walked back to our starting point. And with our clothes all wet and full of sand, we fell exhausted beside each other; she, with her sandy hair, played beside me without a care in the world. Hugging me, kissing my lips and that was the trigger for us to have sex, but not that aggressive or surprising sex, but a more relaxed one, with more touch and finesse.

Later, we fell asleep on the sand, under the moonlight, just as she wanted, until we were surprised by sunlight, announcing the morning. Upon awakening, I realized how dirty our clothes were. We got rid of the salt on our bodies with fresh water and went to my car. I drove her home and after she asked me to please leave her alone, she wrote her phone number on my tie with red lipstick. It surprised me, as I didn't even ask her for it.

I returned to my car and I noticed the seats were wet, because of our clothes' moisture. What would've otherwise bothered me a lot, this time, made me laugh. I was on my way to my apartment, thinking about how much her attitude confused me. That was the fourth tie she dirtied with her lipstick. 'It's the best spot I've ever

94

seen in one of my clothes!' When I arrived at my apartment, I decided to keep the tie with her number and hang it in my closet, next to her blouse, as my only life trophy. 'This is the best night I've had in a long time!' 'She looked beautiful with her wet and sandy hair!' I smiled upon remembering it.

Right at that moment, my cell phone rang, reminding me that I had a girlfriend and that I was about to get married; which, apparently, I had forgotten.

"Hello, love."

"How are you, Lisa?"

"You didn't come last night. What happened?" She asked surprised.

"I was very tired and fell asleep."

"Remember that we have to confirm our reservation at the club on Monday, for our wedding", she said, reminding me of something I'd already stashed away in my memory.

"Ah! Yes, of course love."

# Chapter 7

BECAUSE of that young girl, my wedding was no longer a priority. Truth is, I wasn't sure if marrying Lisa was the right thing to do. But, how could I risk my marriage for something I wasn't even sure where it was going? Something that had no direction, maybe not even a future.

I arrived at my girlfriend's house on Monday and we went to the club to close the contract for our wedding. After doing all that, I simply went to the company office and John's arguments and tips wouldn't stop. I just wanted the day to end, to go home and not have to endure my brother's fights and advice. After I left work, I called Alisha on my way home.

"Hello! How are you, Alisha?"

"Alex! How are you?" she answered, and I could hear she was smiling, but still very surprised to hear my voice. It was as if she didn't remember giving me her number.

"I'm leaving work and wanted to call to hear from you."

"I'm well. And you?"

"Thinking a lot about you", I said, driven by my heart and without fear of her knowing.

"Don't."

"Then, what should I do? I can't get you out of my mind."

"It's not good for you to think so much about me", it was as if she wanted to keep me from having feelings for her.

"Why do you say that, Alisha?"

"It's just that…. no, forget it!"

"What were you going to say?" I was very intrigued. I wanted to know more about her and her mysteries.

"Have you forgotten that you're getting married in a few months?"

"Is that really what you wanted to say? It sounded like you were going to say something else", I was sure there was something else.

"It was just that", reminding me about my wedding.

"No I didn't forget, but if you..."

"Don't say it, Alex. Please don't!" she claimed, halting my impulse.

"But, why are you like that? Are you afraid of something or someone? Why the mystery?"

"Just have fun with me while it lasts. Don't ask for more, please! And don't fall for me", as I heard her speak I felt a lump in my throat. As if she wanted to keep me close; but at the same time, far away from her love. I noticed she was crying. At least, that's what it sounded like.

"That's the problem, I think I already have", my head was exploding in confusion "Can I visit you now?" I risked asking, with a ninety-nine percent certainty in my head that she'd say no.

"Do you think coming to my apartment will change anything?"

"I want to see you!"

"Well, believe it or not... I also want to see you."

"Really?!" I asked, surprised and with my heart rushing. I never expected that answer.

"Yes", she said again without hesitation.

I couldn't believe that was coming out of her lips: I want to see you! It shocked me completely. I changed my course, from going home, to seeing her.

Her apartment door opened, and before me... was the most beautiful woman in the world. She was so beautiful!

"Hello, Alex."

"Hello, my love", I said, like a husband to his wife, after a long workday.

Suddenly, she was stroking my hair. Her left hand grabbed my right hand to lead me to the living room and, suddenly, she began kissing my neck, and then pushed my body into the couch. As she kissed me, she loosened my tie and shirt with sudden movements, breaking some of the buttons. It was as if she wanted to erase that weak and fragile girl image I'd seen at the beach, under the moonlight. She undressed me entirely and I again saw the image of that young girl from before, the one that took charge, the one who bit and overpowered my senses. That Alisha, who liked to feel like she had my whole attention, the one who looked into my eyes letting me know she had the power and she set the rules. In short… the woman I met, full of sensuality and mystery. In short, the woman who transported me to a different world. Once I was under her command, she ran down my chest, slowly, until she reached my penis, making my whole body shake as she sucked it, making me moan with pleasure. The feeling I had was unique; I stroked her hair, staring at the ceiling as my body underwent extremely pleasant cramps. She left my penis to go up to my waist, as if it were a private function. I took off her blouse, leaving her in panties, which I later took off when I rose from the couch, carrying her body and putting my sex on hers. Walking around the living room, stumbling around, we reached the kitchen. We were both shouting due to the intense pleasure. I sat her on the counter, pushing aside some dishes and spread her legs to get lost among them. I put my lips on her vagina, making her cry out with pleasure. The force her legs exerted on my back made me know that their cries were as true as mine. I went up to her neck, brushing our sexes. I went down her neck, and reaching her left breast I bit it gently, aware that she went crazy every time I did. Desperately, she introduced my penis into her vagina; screaming my name, asking me not to stop. She completely clung onto my body like a stamp, biting my lips. She placed her legs on my shoulders, asking me to punish her, without taking her eyes off mine for a second. Right at that moment, I embraced her waist and gazed into her eyes. I placed her on her back as I felt the swing of my penis inside her vagina, I grabbed her hair and her cries grew louder. She asked me to spank her a bit. My body was sweating and her grunting led to mine. She asked for more and more and I kept indulging her desires. I felt like I had a potential nymphomaniac with me.

"My god, I love it, Alex! Keep going, don't stop, please, don't stop", she yelled without rest, holding on the edge of the counter, looking at me over her right shoulder.

I grabbed her hair, and after some spanking I got close to her right ear, and whispered how much I was enjoying the moment. Hearing my voice, whispering softly in her ear, excited her even more. My veins wanted to pop out of my body at that time. We burst into the cry of a splendid feeling. Our bodies were left sweaty and exhausted in a single sigh.

After satiating our cravings and showering each on their own, she decided to cook something for me. I couldn't believe that, since every time we had sex she urged me to leave. We had lunch together like two lovers. I took the opportunity, as we drank some water at that same table, to ask something that took her completely by surprise...

"Alisha, why do you work at the bar?"

"Why do you insist on asking so much about me?" She glanced at me, looking a bit uncomfortable with my question.

"Your mysteries intrigue me. You never talk about yourself or your family", I couldn't help wanting to know more about her. I wanted to examine everything I was experiencing and make a decision in my life.

Right at that moment, I felt like I had the strength to call off my wedding with Lisa and run into her arms, without fearing anything. In response to that question, she paused before answering.

"It's just that… I don't want you to go away yet", she said, changing her face.

"And why would I go away?" I couldn't understand her change of attitude. It was her indecisiveness that didn't allow me to break up with my girlfriend and move on.

"You need to leave, Alex. Please, leave!" again, she was using the easy way out she always relied upon when she felt cornered by my questions.

"Why is it that every time I face you and want to know more about your life, you ask me to leave? Do you live with someone?"

"I told you to go, Alex, please go. Someday, you'll understand, but not now. Go away! If you want, you can call me tomorrow", she said, very agitated and rising from the table to open her apartment door, wanting me to leave.

And again, she eventually threw me out. 'Why the hell does this keep on happening?' 'I don't understand the mystery.' 'What is wrong with this girl?'. 'I don't know how to deal with it.' 'Every time I want to know more is like stabbing her in the chest', my mind shattered into a thousand pieces, trying to find a logical reason for her reactions.

The following day, I went to the gym as usual.

"Hey, Marc."

"How are you doing Alex?" he answered as always, patting me on the back.

"Marc, I want to tell you something... no, forget it."

"Tell me. Don't worry, that's what friends are for."

"Forget it, it doesn't matter."

At the last moment, I decided not to tell Marc what was happening, because since I'd been with the stripper that first time, for him I was no longer going to the bar: according to him, I got what I wanted and left, as I told him I would when I met her. I decided to drop it and for him to not find out how stubborn I was being with the girl. I went to the company later, and when I was already sitting in my office...

"Alex, we need to talk."

"I've told you, John, stop insisting about Alisha."

"It's not her I want to talk about... look at these papers", he handed me over a yellow folder, full of receipts and documents concerning our company.

"What about these papers?" I answered, looking at him, not understanding what he meant.

"We can't keep on pretending like nothing is happening, Alex. Look at those numbers, our company is no longer the same. It isn't paying for itself", he explained very distressed, patting the documents.

"But you told me that Jimmy was working on funding. What happened?"

"You're right, but apparently it's not as easy as we thought. If we continue like this, it'll end very badly."

"What can we do?" I asked confused, as the most experienced in everything relating to the factory was my brother.

"In the meantime, I think we need to decrease the company's and even our own personal expenses. Customers no longer want to invest their money in our skin products", his expression, when he said each word, was of concern. Leaving the folder in my office and asking me to review the documents, he left.

After finishing that hectic day at work and all the worrying, I went back home as usual; but after receiving such discouraging news about my company, my mind was a puzzle. My phone rang as I drove home.

"Hello love", said Lisa, on the other side of the phone. She sounded happy.

"Hello, Lisa", I said, without emotion and annoyed by the bad day I was having.

"Love, I called to tell you that I got the club's confirmation for our wedding today. I have it in my hands right now, it's been signed by the president... It's great, love! The club is ours!" she yelled, very excited. I could imagine her happy face just by listening to her.

"Yes, Lisa, that's great", I said without even flinching, coldly and obviously discouraged.

"But, why did you say it so sadly? Aren't you glad about the news?"

"Yes, love, of course. It's just that John gave me very bad news. But I'm glad you received the confirmation for our wedding."

"But, what did he say? Are you at your apartment, Alex?" she sounded very worried about my comment.

"Yes, I just got here."

"I'm near your house. I'll see you in a few minutes, I'll go and we can talk. See you there, love!" she said, hanging up.

Lisa showed up as I waited for her with a drink.

"Hello love, what's wrong?" she said, holding my neck and kissing me.

"You know, the same, the company isn't coming afloat. Financial companies don't want to work with us. We might have to sell the factory, or worse, lose it."

"Don't worry, love, everything will be alright. Please calm down", she said, placing her hands on my shoulders, trying to cheer me up.

We walked up to my couch. She tried everything to make me feel better. Minutes later, I was feeling so well that from one moment to another, our clothes were on the floor, next to the couch. We ended up having sex, starting on the couch and finishing in the kitchen. She stayed with me and we awoke lying on the furniture.

In the morning, after waking up, I went to the bathroom to take a shower while she was still asleep. As I showered, I thought about the factory's problems. At that moment, the furthest thing from my mind was young Alisha. I was only worried about my family's heritage, the factory where I grew up playing, every time my parents took me with them and where John and I did more than one disaster. That factory meant a lot to me. Besides, it was the only job I knew how to do; the only one I had.

I let my nostalgic thoughts go as I took a towel to wrap it around my waist. I got out of the bath and when I opened the bathroom door, I found myself face to face with my girlfriend. She was holding one of my ties. To be more specific... the one I kept as a trophy in my closet and which had young Alisha's number on it, written in red lipstick. Apparently, she found it when she was trying to hang the clothes that were scattered all over the floor. But now, instead of my usual pants and shirt, there was a different garment; it was crushed, as if it'd endured flamenco dancing and Spanish castanets.

"Can you explain the meaning of this, Alex? Why is there a number written in lipstick on your tie? And what is this woman's blouse doing here?" she asked, with obvious anger, standing in front of me and pointing to the blouse rolled on the ground.

My mind was blank, I could only see my tie hanging on one of her fingers, showing the number. But everything got even worse when she started dialing the number on my phone. When she entered the last digit, the screen showed... Alisha."

"Who's Alisha? I seem to have heard that name before!" she said red with anger and rage. Apparently, she didn't remember the girl, or she'd at least forgotten her name.

At that moment, I had no alibi. I couldn't even think clearly. I kept trying to figure it all out in my head, looking to get out of it. It was cocky of me to keep that shirt and tie in my closet. I think I did, because of how infrequent my fiancée's visits were to my apartment. So I ran to take the phone away from her, and then, try to make up any excuse… it was too late; she moved the phone away, pushing the dial button, hoping to somehow find answers on the other side.

"…?"

"No, this isn't Alex", she said after hearing… I don't know what, at the other side of the phone.

"…?"

"So you're Alisha?!" she walked from side to side, very agitated.

"…?"

"Oh…! I remember you. Right…! You're the girl from the accident. Of course! Alisha! I remember you now. I can't believe this! Who are you really, can you explain please…?"

At that moment, I again ran to her, this time taking the phone away, which fell to the floor after my girlfriend slapped me.

"Alex, please explain! Why do you have the number of the girl you took to your parents' house on your tie, and why was this blouse hanging beside it? And which is evidently of her size?" she shouted angrily, her white skin turning into a reddish color, much brighter than it was a few minutes before and getting that twinkle in her blue eyes, the same that allowed me to know the extent of her anger.

"Are you forgetting it was you who took her?" I answered in cheap defense, without being able to come up with anything else.

"It doesn't matter who did, just explain! You're screwing that girl, aren't you? Of course! She's the book girl, I remember her well. Now everything makes sense: the elevator, the famous accident and all those other stories," she said with tears in her eyes, hitting my chest.

"It's not as you think, Lisa", I took her hands by the wrists, trying to explain everything.

"Of course they are! She answered the phone, knowing it was you", she explained, shaking her arms so I'd let go of her hands, and hitting my chest again, this time harder.

"It's just that… When I took her home, there was no other way for her to give me her number in case there were any complications", without time to think, all my excuses were as cheap as they were absurd.

"Alex, I no longer believe your lies. Enough of your tricks! She could've saved it directly on your phone. You are so stupid! Goodbye…!" she said, weeping inconsolably and slapping my left cheek again.

My girlfriend ran off with the tie and although I tried to stop her, I couldn't, as I was only wearing a towel. 'I'd never seen her act that way.' 'Not like that, so aggressive.' Watching her leave, I ran to get some clothes on. And then I immediately ran after her, hoping she was still close. When I didn't see her anywhere, I took my phone off the floor and got in my car. I called Alisha several times. But for as much as the phone rang, she didn't answer my calls. I tried calling her again, but nothing, no response. Then, I tried calling Lisa and I couldn't contact her either. Rapidly, I thought they may be talking to each other, as Lisa had the tie with her number. I could only think of looking for my girlfriend to try and calm her down. As I drove to my girlfriend's house, where I imagined she'd be, my phone rang.

"Alex, what happened to your girlfriend?" asked Alisha on the other side of the phone, sounding a bit agitated, but definitely not in shock.

"What happened, Alisha?"

"I just talked to you girlfriend… well, no… rather she insulted me endlessly", she said all of this without complaint.

"But, what did she say?" I was very anxious to know what they talked about.

"What she did say, you mean?"

"Wait for me; I'll go to your house. I'll see you in a few minutes", I said, very concerned and without allowing her to refuse.

I detoured to the girl's house, and when I got to her apartment, I imagined I'd find a very worried and upset woman due to what had happened. I went in desperate and anxious to know exactly what they'd talked about, to get a better idea of how to face my girlfriend.

"What did Lisa say exactly?" I asked, without even saying hello, overlooking how gorgeous she looked.

"She just yelled very unpleasant things. She called me slut; she knew I had something to do with you. She basically didn't let me talk. She knew everything that was going on between us, among other things…"

"And what did you say?" I asked, holding my head and walking around.

"Well, from all her questions… the ones I could answer, I answered with the truth. She asked me who I was, actually; how I met you. She said she no longer believed the story of the accident or of that coincidence in the elevator. I ended up telling her what I work in and how we met; but I also told her not to worry about me, as you really love her, and that I'm nothing but a misstep in your life. That the tie with my number and that shirt wouldn't change your love for her."

"Why would you say that, Alisha? And how do you know that's what the fight was about? She told you, didn't she?"

"Alex, I heard it all. The call was still on. There was no reason to keep on lying to your fiancée. We women aren't dumb; we know when there's a truth to be known, even if we want to confirm it with you men. One thing is to know the truth and a different one to accept it", she explained, very calmly.

"But, why the hell would you tell her about you? You could've made up something? I don't know, give her any excuse."

"I told you, I'm not going to become part of your lies or those of anyone in this world. Life has taught me a lot in my time here. If I played along that one time, it was because I didn't know what was happening. I know I'll have to pay for my last lie… but that's something I'll have to carry with for the rest of my life."

"But, what do I do now? How do I get out of this?"

"You'll think of something. Here, the expert in lying is you. Look for her and tell her the truth. I don't know… make up something, but don't lose her. Now go!" she said, practically pushing me to my girlfriend and walking me to the door.

"Truth is, if I'm honest, I don't even know what to think. I just know you've become more than a misstep for me. I'm so confused! So much that I no longer know if I should get married or not…!" I wanted her to tell me not to get married. I was willing to do anything for her.

"I'm sure you're just confused. Now go and look for her", I didn't understand why she kept on insisting that I stay away from her. Why didn't she want me with her?

"I don't want to go now, I want to stay here, with you", I couldn't avoid my stubbornness. I just wanted to be with her, despite what was happening.

"You want to, but you can't, Alex. So, please, leave and fix things with your girlfriend. Please, try not to involve me in your affairs again. Goodbye", she said, holding the door with her left hand and throwing me out, as she always did.

In the end, I had no choice but to go and try to find Lisa. I got to my girlfriend's house and for as much as I called her, she never came out. I could only imagine she wasn't there, perhaps she went to her parents' house. I hid in my apartment, waiting for her to communicate with me or come to get me. For as much as I tried to find her, I couldn't. As I thought of all the things that had happened in a single day, I fell asleep, already with a few drinks in my body. I woke up the next day, conscious that it hadn't all been a dream. That day, I didn't go to the gym or work, with the sole purpose of finding a way to fix the mess I made. Hours went by and I still couldn't contact my girlfriend, so I went to my parents' house and asked about her. To my surprise, my family already knew what had happened.

111

"Son, what the hell is wrong with you?" yelled my mother angrily; while Sara and my father only listened.

"Mom, this is between us, please don't meddle in..." a slap interrupted my sentence.

"You don't talk to me that way. Do you think that just because you're a man you can disrespect me?" she said, standing in front of me, with that mature woman strength and unique temperament.

My father and Sara didn't move a finger to stop my mother. They feared her as much as I did. We all respected her and her way of saying things, making it hard to contradict her. Even my father wouldn't take a step without her approval.

"You're right mom, sorry", I said, putting my head down.

"I'm not going to let a child of mine ruin his life for a nobody. I'd rather die than see that", she yelled, very convinced of her words.

Then my father took my shoulder and I pulled me away from her, walking me to the exit, while my mother yelled for me to get out of her house, that she didn't want to see me until I stopped seeing that brat.

"But, son, how could you get involved with that girl?" said my father, with his tired steps and low voice.

My mother's scolding was so extreme; that she ended up throwing me out. I couldn't believe she'd talked to me that way. It was as if I'd just spoken to Lisa's mom.

'Why did Alisha confirm everything to Lisa?'. 'Why couldn't she deny everything?'. I tried communicating again with Lisa, unsuccessfully. I went to a bar and started drinking crazily, without having anyone to talk to. I wanted to call my friend, Marc and tell him everything, but then I stopped to think of how little I'd told him about the girl. What was happening to me, I didn't even want to tell my best friend. So I decided to get drunk alone. Drown my sorrows; think about everything I was going through. Neither Lisa nor her family nor mine wanted to hear my excuses.

The next day, there was a knock at my office door. This time I had to endure my brother, John's scolding. Since Lisa had made that whole fuss with Alisha, I had become the bad guy. I couldn't get anyone to forgive me. My mother was even more offended than my girlfriend. Her scolding wouldn't stop. She called me constantly, only to insult and advise me. She defended Lisa more than her own mother. I came to think that she was her daughter and I was the degenerate that had caused her pain.

To all this, days passed and Friday came. I insisted on communicating with my girlfriend. After so much persistence, she picked up my last call, which already meant something to me.

"What do you want, Alex?" she said in a loud and very intimidating tone.

"I want us to talk, Lisa. Please, let me explain."

"What for…? So you can lie to me again? So I'll fall back into your arms as if nothing had happened? No, Alex, I'm tired of your lies."

"I want to apologize, Lisa. Listen to me, I beg of you!"

"You and I have nothing to talk about. If you want, you can stay with that cheap whore. Don't look for me anymore, goodbye!" she hung up. She seemed very determined to end what we had.

That was my last conversation with her, before a few more weeks went by.

# Chapter 8

THROUGHOUT the last month, despite everything, I kept on meeting with young Alisha; I only needed a word from her to give up on everything and stay with her... she never did. Anyway, I was still obstinately into her. Our nights of passion were still confusing to me. But I kept accepting her crumbs, like someone who got medicine every four hours to keep their fever down. My family was still reluctant to accept my relationship with her. My mother persisted with her calls. According to her, I couldn't leave Lisa for the bar brat. My brother was the one who told her I was still seeing her. I didn't understand why my brother was behaving like that with me. Sometimes, when we argued in the office, I felt like reminding him of his past; but, that would've been feeding the fire. He still didn't know who Alisha was friends with.

The only person who, at least didn't scold me and who actually answered my calls, was my sister, Sara, who even though wasn't happy with what I was doing, at least didn't judge me so harshly. I no longer had any arguments to convince Lisa to come back. I tried everything, until I lose all hope of her forgiving me. Then, I decided, tired of begging and insisting for her to get back together with me... not to chase her anymore.

My desire for the girl from the bar was still as strong as when I saw her that first day. I returned to the bar every Friday. When she was done with her show, I picked her up at the parking lot, as I'd been doing in recent weeks. I remember it was a cold and foggy night. She looked so beautiful with her scarf around her neck! As we drove to her apartment in my car, she made me reroute, to go to a shop and have some tea. We walked to the shop, and truth be told, walking with her was a luxury. Everyone turned to stare at us... sorry! To stare at her, even though her body was covered by a brown jacket, and a matching scarf, with white squares that highlighted the sparkle in her brown eyes, she looked gorgeous! When we left, we got in the car and threw our coats in the back seat. Blaming the early hours and the darkness that reigned that night at the parking lot... she touched my right thigh with her left hand, making small strokes, and giving me a peculiar look. Despite her touch, I started the car, looking to get out of there and head to her apartment. Suddenly... she let go of my thigh, to take the keys from the ignition, turning off the engine. So we stayed there, without moving an inch.

"Would you dare...?" she whispered, glancing at me sideways.

"But, Alisha, we're at a parking lot! Someone could come out of the store and see us....or someone could

116

come", I knew exactly what she meant. It was one of the few things I understood from her, the way she asked for sex.

"It's 2:00am, Alex. So, is that a no?" she whispered, as she played with my car keys with her index finger throwing her body against mine, to kiss my lips again and again, slowly; she enjoyed blackmailing my feelings.

I looked around the place and, upon seeing how empty and far away we were from the store, being at one of the darkest and foggiest parts of the parking lot, her persistence forced my weakness to take her in my arms biting her fleshy lower lip. She immediately began to undo my belt buckle, after unbuttoning each of my white shirt's buttons and kissing my chest. She unzipped my pants, taking my member in her right hand and leading her mouth to it. I stroked her hair with my right hand and, occasionally, her buttocks, lifting her tight dress, putting my hand under her thong, while she kept on stroking and sucking my penis. A feeling ran through my veins, forcing me to leave her hair to place my hands on the wheel, squeezing it tightly. As always, she controlled everything that was happening between us. I daresay she controlled her orgasm and mine, because she left my penis right on time. Crossing her right leg over my body, she sat in front of me. I managed, as I could, to lean the sit backwards, settling in and raising her dress a little above her waist. She pulled my hands up against my seat's head cushion, whispering in my ear:

"Don't move, bad boy!"

She grabbed my belt, tying my hands up there, just as she did that time in her bathroom. I could've released my hands whenever I wanted, as her ties were very weak. With her scarf, she blindfolded me, leaving me in the dark. All of this made my blood calm down a little. Her erotic games scared me; as it was clear she'd read "50 Shades of Grey", but at the same time I trusted her so much, I didn't mind playing her 50 shades. With her left hand, she took my penis to sink it, through one side of her thong, into her vagina already moistened by my touch. Her movements over me, pulled all sorts of whimpers and phrases from me. As our pleasure increased, she bit my lip, resting her hands on the seat. Minutes later, my desperation apparently forced her to release my hands. I wrapped her waist, without wasting time, contorting her body with mine and bit her left nipple, with constantly yet limited waist movements. She removed my blindfold, to see my eyes and wrap me with her gaze; through it she told me she was coming. She bit her lips and then bit mine as well, afterwards, she screamed my name, again and again; forcing me, with her blackmail, to yell hers. With my hands on her waist, under her dress and wearing out our lips, we let a long side escape from inside, which made both her strength and mine run out. Our crazy pleasure, made me forget where we were. I only realized it after we were done, exhausted form playing a game I'd never played before and in which, by losing part of your fluids, you can get to be a happy winner.

"Alisha, you're going to drive me crazy with your follies", she had the same expression she'd had that time in the elevator.

"Will it always be my fault, Alex?" she whispered, with the same look that characterized her and that sarcasm I liked so much in her. Those half-smiles she had so much trouble to complete, maybe because she was afraid of telling me she was crazy for me... I don't know, I liked to think so.

"My God, Alisha... I think... if you could do it in a church, I could…; at least I'd think about it, so I wouldn't accept such madness", I was aware of the power she had over me.

"Don't worry, I'll keep it in mind", she said, glancing sideways on the ride home.

"Would you really dare to propose that? Don't play with me", I looked at her, also sideways, with my hands on the wheel.

"You can always refuse. It isn't my fault that you can't decide", again hiding her irony with that unique look and smile.

After my dose of sex, as she called our meetings, I dropped her off at home, after my persistence of trying to stay with her. It was something that, though nothing changed, I kept trying. A few days later, one morning, my phone rang.

"What's wrong with you, Alex? You haven't been to the gym" asked Blondie.

"I've been very busy, Marc. But don't worry. I'll get dressed and I'll be there in a few minutes; I need exercise again", I said, shaking my body when I jumped out of bed, still rubbing my eyes.

"Hey Blondie, how are you?"

119

"How are you doing, Alex? You're losing weight. That wedding is eating you up even before you get married. Wait until you do and you'll know what it is to get really big. Just an example: your brother, hahaha!" he screamed, throwing a left hook into my liver, as a greeting, with his typical laugh.

"Marc, I have to tell you something...: there won't be a wedding", I said, sitting on the bench, as I put on my exercise gloves.

"What do you mean there won't be a wedding, Alex?! Explain this to me slowly."

"There are a lot of things you don't know yet, Blondie."

"Ok, tell me what's going on! What is it that I don't know?" he asked curiously.

Among our workouts I told my friend everything. Sure! Omitting a few irrelevant details.

"That girl has muddled my life. Now, everything revolves around her. As you can see, I've even forgotten my exercises."

"But, Alex, how many times did you tell me you wouldn't see her again and that it was her who kept calling you and looking for you? I thought you trusted me."

"It's just that, you said you were tired of my adventures and I didn't want you to see me like the old trick-less wolf you said I was, that's why I made up all those cheap stories and acted strong before you."

"Truth is, Alex, I don't know what to say; but my advice as your friend, is that you stay away from her as much as you can. Remember the power those women have; it's as if they did a masters in what they do. You know I'm not your girlfriend's best friend, but I don't want you to screw up your life either. Remember what almost happened a while ago."

"There's more, Blondie… she's friends with the redhead. Can you imagine if my brother finds out. It'd be like putting a noose around my own neck. For my brother, Rosa doesn't even work at the bar."

"Don't tell me she's Rosa's friend?! Are you telling me a soap opera or is this your life, Alex?" he was astonished, mouth open as soon as I mentioned the redhead.

"I didn't want to tell you about Rosa, because of what happened between you and my brother."

"I know, Alex, but you know I never had anything with Rosa; it was because of her I stopped going to the bar, to keep my friendship with your brother and my relationship with my girlfriend, even though I wasn't able to convince John."

"I know, Marc; you don't have to prove that to me, don't worry. You're still my childhood friend for something. Well, let's get to what we came for; I'll see how to fix my life drama. It isn't worth remembering the past nor that fight between you two."

We left the gym and I was driving to my office. I couldn't deny that, having told Blondie, was a huge relief, it was comforting. 'I think Blondie is right, I should stay away from her.' 'But, how the hell do I do that'. 'Lisa doesn't deserve this.' 'It hurts to be in a fight with my mother.' 'You're losing your family, Alex!'.

'What the hell is wrong with you?'. I kept on mistreating my mind. When suddenly, a two-tone ring in my phone caught my attention:

Message received:

[Hi, Alex, I want to talk to you]

I read my phone screen. 'Oh, my God, Lisa!'. Seeing that text was a huge surprise, after she'd rejected me so many times. Despite the time that had gone by, I still couldn't figure out what I meant to the girl from the bar; as she increasingly confused my mind with her ups and downs. We had a relationship without heads or tails. So, that message from Lisa made me ponder a few things. With just one word from the girl's mouth, I would've dared to ignore that message. I took the phone in my hands and called Lisa.

"I need us to talk, Alex", she said on the other side of the line.

"Ok, love. If you want, I can go to your house right now."

"Not today, I'll see you tomorrow afternoon."

"But I can go to your department right now, love", I said, willing to start again and forget the stripper, deciding to resume my life.

"I'd rather it be tomorrow", she stated, leaving me in the dark, not knowing what she wanted to talk about, although I sensed she wanted to get back together with me, due to the soft tone of her voice.

"Ok, love, see you tomorrow", I said, loving and hoping to start again, following Marc's advice.

After that call, I thought for a long time. Truth was, I'd lost all hope with her. The day came in which I had to talk to Lisa and fix our differences.

"Hello, love", I was surprised to see her open her apartment door. She was wearing a pink baby doll with ruffles on her hips and a deep cleavage. That definitely told me she wanted me back.

"How are you, Alex? Come in and sit", she pulled by left hand to take me to her couch, where there were two drinks and a scented candle on the coffee table.

"You know, Lisa, I'm not well without you. I want to apologize for my mistake..."

"I don't want to hear anything, Alex. Right now I just want to be with you", she silenced me and I could no longer control my desire of making her mine; I sought to forget the stripper in her, for everything to go back to what it was before she appeared in our life; return to my perfect like, the one I should've never left.

"Let's toast to this moment, Alex!"

We took our glasses and moistened our lips with French red wine. I wrapped her in my arms, wanting to show her how sorry I was for my actions. I kissed her lips and she kissed mine. Her light body settled into the couch and I thoroughly caressed her skin. She, as desperate as I was, unbuttoned my shirt and everything else, as I only took off her panties. In front of me, with her legs over my shoulders, my waist moved constantly, as constantly as her screams. I took her calves with my hands, to see how my penis entered her vagina. She looked at me, her eyes almost closed and with her hands clutching the couch. I watched her head twisting backwards. Our desire was so great, we couldn't keep going; I ended up laying languidly with a long breath that stirred my lungs.

"Alex, I want you to stop seeing that girl and for us to go ahead with our wedding", she said, taking my hands and staring right at me.

"Love, I promise you, I will, you don't need to worry about her anymore. Fortunately, I realized my mistake on time. I want to promise you I won't go back to the bar and that, starting today, I will only have eyes for you."

"I hope so, Alex; remember that our families are also suffering", she kissed my lips softly.

Hours went by and we had sex again in the morning, leaving our second breath in her bed. I ran home early to change and go to work. I didn't think it necessary to go to the gym that day, as with what I'd done, I'd burned more calories than I usually did there.

Hours and days went by… and Friday arrived. I went to the gym early in the morning; more to tell Marc I was following his advice than to exercise.

"How are you doing, Alex?"

"Marc, I need to tell you something", I said, inviting him to sit at the bench with me.

"Don't tell me you're marrying the girl from the bar. Please let me be your best man, hahaha!" he said, mocking me, when he saw me smiling.

"No, not that man! I want to tell you that I'm following your advice. I was able to fix things with my girlfriend, so our wedding is still on", I felt very sure of wanting to forget the dancer to try and give everything to my relationship with Lisa and my family.

"Then, get me out of the best man list!" he said bragging, as he was sure Lisa wouldn't want him at our wedding.

"I'm serious, Blondie."

"I know, Alex. Sorry, I am really happy for you. I think it's the best decision you've made. Even if I can't go to your wedding, I wish you well."

"I know Marc, I'm very sure of that."

"Alex, enough of your stories, we came here to sweat. So, get up from that bench and take these dumbbells", Blondie loved the smell of sweat: not for nothing, he had one of the most toned bodies at the gym; he took our routine very seriously.

I finished my morning routine. When I arrived at work, I told my brother all about Lisa and me; of my decision about ending my relationship with the bar girl and of how I was willing to carry on with my wedding plans.

Just as I had sworn to myself, I spent two Fridays without attending the bar. Everything was going well between my girlfriend, our family and me. I can't deny that sometimes I felt tempted to call the stripper or send her a text, just as I expected her to do it. But my effort to not fail my girlfriend and my mother again, was stronger this time than my desire to see her again.

Alisha, despite having my cell number, never called me or texted me. Something that puzzled me about her, but which at the same time I was thankful of for obvious reasons.

# *Chapter 9*

**IT WAS** the third Friday after my reconciliation with Lisa. I was still as convinced of not going to see Alisha, like the previous two Fridays. That day, after leaving work, I knew I shouldn't attend the bar as much as I did the day I met her. I was driving to my apartment; but this time, I decided to get some flowers and a good wine for my fiancée. Even though we had no plans of getting together that night, I wanted to surprise her. I diverted to get what I was looking for. When I was returning from getting the wine, I was surprised when I saw something as I walked back to my BMW..., 'I can't believe it!', 'this must be a joke!'. They were going into a restaurant called Roma Rose, across the street...; I placed the flowers and bottle of wine in the back of my car, got in, and when I was turning around stopped in front of the establishment, confirming what I couldn't believe with my own eyes. From my car I watched... a handsome, well dressed blonde man sitting at one of the restaurant tables. From my car, that was all I managed to see of him. I wanted to jump out of my seat and punch him endlessly, I saw him and couldn't understand it… Alisha was sitting in front of him. 'Is this a fucking joke or is it true?!'. 'How can this be?!'. He took her hands, I saw it. My mind was making all kinds of conjectures. I pushed the accelerator all the way down, to ran way burning its tires. I didn't know if she'd recognized my car in front of the restaurant. 'Damn it, it was her!'. 'What the hell, Alex, forget her, now!' My brain was a ticking time bomb. I arrived home, made myself a strong drink without no ice; I wanted it to peel down my throat and maybe then I'd be able to forget what my eyes saw. It was about 10:00 pm and I was still drinking, in the living room, tormenting my mind; also forgetting the surprise I'd planned for give Lisa. 'Maybe it was nothing and they're just friends.' 'It could be my imagination'. 'Is she sleeping with him?!' 'Maybe I should ask for an explanation'. 'Why the hell do I care, if I already decided to forget her?' I saw her in each of my drinks. 'I need to know!' I got my keys and headed to the bar. I arrived a few minutes before her show. I heard how they announced her presentation. I decided to wait for her in the parking lot and not see her show that night; I needed to calm my anxiety. I took a deep breath and calmed my emotions. I decided not to say anything of what I'd seen; I only wanted to see what reaction she would give and how far she'd take her hypocrisy. 'I need to clear things up and forget about her.' 'Focus on my relationship with Lisa'. 'I can't throw my marriage away because of her', I thought, while I waited in the parking lot. I was very surprised not to see Rosa's car in her usual spot, but I didn't give it much importance, as I knew the person I wanted to see was there. I decided to wait, determined to tell her everything I thought if she confirmed my suspicion. I saw her come into the parking lot. 'Wow! She looks beautiful!', I sighed when I saw her walking in front of me. She was more beautiful than ever. 'I don't know how I'm going to clear my doubts.' 'Did she dress like that for him?!' I tormented myself.

"What are you doing here, Alex?" she was very surprised to see me there waiting, after not calling or seeing her in more than two weeks.

"Where you expecting someone else?" I asked, faking a smile.

"No, why?", she was still surprised. I noticed it in her voice.

"It's just that, as I didn't see Rosa's car, I can assume you weren't expecting me..." I didn't know if she could sense the irony in my words or if my acting was any good.

"Well, yes, I am expecting someone... a taxi, the one that should already be here", she said unhurried and looking everywhere.

For a moment, I thought she would mention the man who was accompanying her at that restaurant whose name I'd like to forget. From that moment, the Rome Rose had entered the list of places I'd never visit again in my life.

"What happened with Rosa? Why don't I see her car?" I was trying to seem as calm as possible and I think I was managing it, though inside, my blood was boiling.

"She's solving something for me. She took the night off", it was one of the longest conversations I'd had with her. I was surprised she was answering all my questions without revealing anything.

"I can take you", I couldn't even imagine that the alleged taxi she was waiting for was actually that man. Otherwise, I wouldn't have been able to sleep at all that night, thinking she'd be with him.

Without complaint, she accepted my proposal. While we were in the car, I tried to find a way to ask her about the man who was with her at the Rome Rose; when suddenly and perhaps without suspecting my true intentions, she looked into my eyes and said:

"Alex, tomorrow will be a very special day for me. I'd like you to be there with me. I want you to come… I was about to text you", she said, completely taking me by surprise.

'No, not now, Alisha, please.' 'I can't fall into your game again.'

At that moment, she looked back and saw the bouquet in my car:

"Is that for me, Alex?" she said, turning to see me and taking it in her hands.

"Ah… yes, they are for you, Alisha! I wanted to surprise you tonight, but turns out that I was the one who got a surprise."

"Thank you so much, what a nice touch! I love them! They're beautiful" And, why did you say you were surprised?"

"No… it's just that you're so beautiful! Those gardenias are nothing compared to how beautiful you are today", truly, I was beginning to forget the promise I'd made to my girlfriend and family.

"Thanks Alex."

"And what's that special thing tomorrow, Alisha?" I didn't want to erase her smile, as she asked me that and smelled the flowers. She was so beautiful! Oh God!

"It's a day that I possibly won't ever repeat. You'll know in due course", I was very intrigued and not understanding the ever in her sentence.

'It'd be wrong.' 'Why does she want to be with me on that special day?'. 'Just leave her and go, Alex,' I thought when I stopped in front of her building.

I couldn't leave without clearing my doubts. We got off the car. She was carrying the flowers in her hands, while I held the bottle of wine. Even though she never showed signs of rejecting me and actually looked rather complacent with me, before my decision got even more complicated:

"Alisha, there's something I want to talk to you about?, I said, as we were walking through her apartment door.

At that moment, she placed her hand on my lips and with a very soft voice and looking into my eyes, said:

"Why so lost?! Bad boy!"

I tried answering, but she silenced me again, and then kissed me.

I, in her presence, was always a very weak man. I was like a chocolate bar under the sun! A lit candle where there was no light. I was carried away by her kiss and by how beautiful she was that night. When I tried talking about the subject, suddenly she began taking off my tie and stroking my hair. At that moment, I could think of nothing else but to make her mine. Gone were all the reasons why I went to see her that night. I proceeded to remove every clothe item from her body, leaving her completely naked. She didn't leave any on my body either and we both ended up wrapped together in a game of passion and desire. In an instant, she took me to the couch and laid her body on mine. The couch became smaller with each of our caresses. As she kneeled on my waist, with my penis in her vagina, moving her waist with a unique style and sensuality, in that climax of intense pleasure, I carried her on my waist and tried to take her to what, in my opinion, was the room, pushing her body against the door. I tried opening it with my right hand, while I kissed and bit her lips; I tried opening it, again and again... it was useless because it was locked. She, with a turn, led me back to the couch, where it had all began. She leaned on a corner of the couch, with her arms on the couch. I stood behind her, with my penis in her vagina I was. Her moans were the nicest ones I'd heard. I took her waist with my left hand and her soft her with my right. As I pulled her hair, her moans were music to my ears. Along with her groans, I heard her say...

"Harder, my love!" the same phrase over and over again. I heard that "my love" leave her lips for the first time, instead of Alex, it was as if she'd made the last payment of a heart she'd been paying for in small installments and now she was taking it with her that night. Hearing that was very special to me, as if I finally knew the reason why I'd gone to see her that night. I didn't know if it was the repressed desire we had for not having seen each other for weeks, but that day, we let it all go. We took our bodies to the limit, there wasn't a corner of the living room in which we didn't play God; bringing our carnal desire to life. With our bodies, sweaty and moaned, turned into sighs, we ended up exhausted in the couch, one beside the other, holding each other in a single body. That petulant child had changed. For the first time she'd said 'my love'! Something that after all the time I'd seen her, she'd never said. However, laying there, after such a satisfying moment, the reason why I'd actually gone to see her that night came to mind; to clear my doubts! Perhaps to say goodbye forever!

"My love, I'll take a shower and I'll be back", she whispered, as she left leaving one last kiss on my chest.

She said 'love' again. It was as if she knew the reason why I was there and didn't want to hear it.

'Did she recognize my car in front of the restaurant?' 'Does she know that I saw them?'

"My love, do you want me to make you something?" she said as she came out of the bathroom.

'Again that phrase!'

"I could use a coffee, as I uncork the bottle of wine and we toast together", I said, without even thinking it.

"I don't drink alcohol, darling", she said as she went into the kitchen.

'What's wrong with this woman? Darling!'. 'She called me that?!'. 'She works in a bar and doesn't drink alcohol'. 'She's should definitely be studied', my mind was a chess game.

During my shower, so many things went through my head...! 'I don't know if I can live without seeing her again.' 'I can't fail my girlfriend now'. 'My family, hers...' 'How will I face all of this?' I wasn't even thinking about that man, after the time I was having. I couldn't think about what has happening between them. I got out of the bathroom and the coffee was already on the table. I waited for the right time to tell her I was marrying Lisa and wouldn't see her again. My priority was no longer knowing about that man, but to find a way to get away from her. I filled my lungs with air to tell her of my decision; but, as it always happened to me... I thought of something to ask.

"Alisha, I have a doubt in my mind. Why, despite having made love in so many places in your apartment and outside of it, have we ever done it in your room? Why is this so…?"

"Remember what I told you several times, Alex?" she looked into my eyes and placed a glass of water she was drinking on the table.

"What do you mean, Alisha?"

"That someday you'll ask the wrong question... because that question you just asked me, Alex, is the wrong question. You knowing the answer involves a lot of things. Do you really want to know why we haven't made love in that room?" she asked, still looking at me.

"Yes, I do", I said, without thinking it twice. Her face changed. She was no longer that woman from hours before. She made so many pauses to say or clarify something, it scared me.

"First, I need to make a few things clear, Alex."

"You're scaring me with your mysteries. What can be so weird or special about that room?" I ignored her fears.

"First, if we go in there, questions will arise I'll feel obliged to respond. After you know the answers, you may leave and what we have may end. You'd also understand a lot of my attitudes and mood swings, of which you've already asked me several times. If you're willing to face my whole truth and reality, I'll open that door, although you do have the choice of us continuing as we have until now: having sex and carrying on with what we have until you get married or I'm no longer here; but it will be difficult for you to not ask something if we enter that room; truth is, I don't think you'd refrain", she said restless and with both hands on the table.

All her mysteries puzzled me even more. I really didn't know if I wanted everything to end. My head was generating all kinds of thoughts, but my curiosity beat my reasoning and I ended up saying:

"I want to go in and know why, according to you, you're hiding your life behind that door."

"Sorry… give me a minute, please", apparently she was expecting a no from me.

In that minute, she collapsed, hugging that door's handle.

"What's the matter, Alisha...? Why are you like that? If you prefer it, we don't have to go in! I don't want this to be a sacrifice for you. I'd rather not know anything?" seeing how her skin changed color scared me, and her face was different.

135

"It's fine, Alex, excuse me. Sooner or later you'll leave me; it'll be better if it's sooner. It'll be better for both of us."

"But, what's wrong…? If you don't want to, you don't have to open that door. Forget my question." She suddenly opened that door, took a few steps forward and she was already inside the room. I had to take two more steps than her, to be at her side. When she turned on the light… I swear I'd never seen anything like it in my life. Seeing that room in the first few minutes left me perplexed. My head began to generate all kinds of questions, when I saw all those clippings on the walls. My surprise was so but, I started walking around the room. Its four walls were like one huge one, with so many newspaper and magazine clippings. There were… I don't know how many classic ballet dancer outfits, first place trophies and personal pictures. But there was something that caught my attention; on one of the walls, there were only four newspaper clippings. As I approached the wall, I noticed that they spoke of an accident in which three people were involved, two women and one man. One of the two women was… Alisha. Due to my surprise, I'd completely forgotten about the girl. Turning my head, I saw her shattered, pouring her soul out, sitting next to the bed, with both arms on her knees and her head resting on her palms. I approached her, trying to comfort her. As she said, several questions came to mind, I didn't even know how or where to start. I placed my hand on her shoulder, sitting next to her, unable to ask anything. I simply wanted to stop her from crying. I still couldn't believe what my eyes were seeing, after about fifteen minutes in the room. Once she was calmer, and without tears in her eyes, my concerns came to life.

"But, what is all this, Alisha?" I asked, looking everywhere.

"This is my personal space! Of joys, sometimes due to all my success as a dancer; and often, of pain, due to the accident. There are days in which I can spend hours here, crying and smiling at times."

"Explain the ballerina costumes. Those trophies, what are they?" I was still very confused.

"It's a long story, Alex. That's why I always feared bringing you home. I didn't want the time to come in which you'd ask all of this."

"It doesn't matter, Alisha, I want to know everything. I see you dressed as a ballerina and with trophies in your hands. It interested me" I was looking for answers to my questions.

I saw her hands began to sweat before she began her story.

"Alex, first of all I want you to know that, what I'm about to tell you, is very hard for me to say. And I don't care if after knowing it you don't want to see me anymore and would, therefore, want to leave. If you want, I'll accept it with resignation and conscious of my responsibility."

"Don't say that, Alisha, please", I was sure that after all that, I wouldn't be able to leave her.

"Those ballerina costumes, medals and trophies you see there... they're part of my dream. I was a ballet dancer; it was my wish since I was very young. My biggest ambition was going to come true this year, as I'd be in a very important theater play. Then tragedy struck, truncating my chance. I was diagnosed with kidney failure, so always I have to get dialysis to treat my blood. I fell into such a deep depression, I tried to kill myself by cutting my wrists; although I only managed to cut the right and before I bled to death, my friend Rosa arrived, saving my life", she wouldn't stop crying as she spoke.

"I'm sorry, love, I don't know what to say, after what you just told me. But, that accident, what does it mean?"

"Do you see that woman next to me in that accident? That's my adoptive mother. The woman who raised me from when I was thirteen."

When I asked about the accident, I noticed it was hard for her to start talking about her mother. She took a deep breath before continuing her story.

"My mother was determined to donate one of her kidneys so I could fulfill my dream, participating in that Broadway play. After all the effort we made to bring my mother, from my country, so she could be my donor, fate played a second round. After the compatibility analysis, which unfortunately was negative for donor, because she wasn't my biological mother, we were driving home when suddenly someone rammed the taxi we were in, killing the taxi driver and leaving my mother, Clara in a coma... sorry, Alex. While I, whom God should've left in a coma, and not her, only suffered minor scratches. My mother had been in a coma for a week and after some studies the doctor told me she'd need an operation, in case she woke up from the coma, she'd suffered liver damage due to the accident. I cursed God, both for the taxi driver's death and for my mother's state. Days went by and my mother still wasn't improving; and I continued with my treatments. My Rosa convinced me to quit my job as a hotel receptionist and work at the bar, just for a while, to be able to cover my mother's and my medical expenses. I couldn't even think of my kidney operation, I only thought of my mother's health. Because of my health, I couldn't work at the bar for more than one day a week and I kept my hotel job three days a week.

One day when I was visiting my mother, as I prayed to God for her health, after cursing Him, kneeling at the foot of her bed, I took her hand and surprisingly, she awoke from the coma. After some medical checkups and spending a few weeks in recovery, she seemed to be doing well; she talked to me, despite her critical condition. It broke my heart when she said:

"My darling, I'm sorry..."

"Don't talk, mom, rest", I said, fearing her condition would worsen.

"My love, I'll have enough time to rest. I want to apologize for not being able to give you my kidney."

"I'm sorry Mommy. If I hadn't brought you to this country, this wouldn't have happened. Please forgive me..."

"Never say that, Alisha. Don't even think about it, I forbid you! We all have a destiny in this life and this is mine. I know I'm going to die, but I will do so calmly, if my Alisha lives her life in peace with herself."

"You'll be fine, mom. We'll be together again, as before."

"My daughter, don't try to deceive me or yourself. We both know I won't live to be with you. Alisha, my daughter, I only want to ask you for something and I want you to do it for me."

"Mommy, please, don't talk", I said crying, unable to console her, knowing how weak her health was.

"I want you to promise me you'll live every day of your life as if it were your last. Enjoy life while you can. Don't let anybody tell you what to do and what not to do. Be yourself. Promise me you'll live your life to the fullest, that your illness won't be an excuse to get depressed, to feel sorry for yourself. I don't want you to try and take your life again. Remember that if you're still alive, after trying it that first time, it's because you have a mission to fulfill in this world. A kidney will come for you, when you least expect it. Promise me, please!"

"I promise, Mom, I swear my life will be as I want it to be. I don't care if that donor comes or not. Each second of each of my days will be special. I'll live it to the fullest, mommy, I promise!"

"Remember, Alisha, though I'm not your biological mother, you were always the daughter I never had. The one I always wanted and which my belly denied me. I asked God so much for her, that she brought me the best daughter in the world in a different way. I never imagined that the girl I looked so much for in me, came as she did."

"But, what happened to your biological mother, Alisha?" my eyes were watery as I interrupted her story.

"That's something I don't want to remember, please. Don't make me talk about her, I beg you. I beg you, don't ask about her."

"Sorry, my love. But, so what happened to the lady who raised you?"

"Alex, that was the last conversation I had with my mother. I still remember her as if it was now. My mother awoke from a coma that day, only to tell me and teach me how to appreciate and live my life. She died holding my hand... sorry, Alex; I will never be able to forget that, in a way, she gave her life for me. I've always felt guilty about my mother's death, for bringing her here to die. Apart from Rosa, who also couldn't give me her kidney due to her incompatibility. My mother traveled from the Dominican Republic, my country, to give me what no one else has wanted to give me... a new lease on life. And that's what made me believe more in my mother's last words. When she said, "live every day of your life as if it were your last", she made me think that fate didn't want me to live longer than necessary. So I lost all hope of finding a donor; but also, thanks to my mother's life lesson, now I appreciate every second of each day I wake up alive."

I'm so sorry, Alisha", I couldn't find a way to comfort her, rather than to shelter her body with mine and dry her tears whenever she cried.

Sitting beside her and not knowing how to respond to this revelation, I waited for her to recover her strength and asked when she was calmer.

"Truth is, I still don't understand. Why would you say I'll stop seeing you, leave you, Alisha?"

141

"It's just that I still haven't told you..." she said, pausing, as if doubting to tell me the rest.

"What, Alisha?" I couldn't find a reason to leave her from her story.

"I didn't meet you by accident, Alex… finding you didn't happen by chance."

"I don't understand, love, what do you mean?"

"Rosa had told me about you and your money."

"Then, it was all for money?" I didn't understand her confession, as she never took a penny from me.

"Yes, it was, Alex."

"Why me? Why me? Why not another businessmen from those who gave you more money and were richer than me? There's something I don't understand. If it was all for money, then why did you never accept a dollar from me?" I was very surprised because of what she had just said, so I released her body and got out of bed.

"Because, according to Rosa, you never skipped the bar on Fridays and that was the day I worked", she stood up from the bed and placed her hands on my chest.

"So what's all this then?"

"I only looked for you to take advantage of you, to get money for my mother's operation and to save her life. Also, because you looked like the wealthy businessman who crashed into us and who days later got out of prison. I thought you were all the same, who got anything they wanted with their money and influence. Also, because I stopped believing in men and started hating each of them. But… days later when I was about to touch the subject of money with you, my mother died, giving me that life changing advice. Therefore, there was no reason to talk about money."

"I can't believe it, Alisha, all this time you were mocking my feelings. I can't believe you saw me as a way out… that you looked for me to avenge your grudge against someone else in me. And my feelings, what about then? They're not worth it?" I removed her hands off my chest, in one sudden movement.

"I know you have the right to say that and much more. I know I don't deserve your forgiveness, my love; but, after my mother died, nothing mattered to me; I started falling in love with you, of the attentions you gave to me, your way of being, your insistence on seeing me... I started noticing you weren't like the others. I saw something special in you", she was trying to convince me that she loved me.

"I don't believe anything, Alisha. You only saw what's good for you. After trying to manipulate me for your purposes, now it turns out that you love me! You know what I think?... You're a calculative woman and only approached me for the money and your thirst for revenge, hoping to attack, as my brother said", I yelled, showing him my truths and the conception I had of her.

"I don't expect you to forgive me, my love. I know I had my motives, but that doesn't justify me following you with that purpose. But I swear I really did fall in love with you, I swear! I love you and now it doesn't hurt to tell you, my love, even when I know I'm going to lose you."

"You've damaged my life. Maybe you're right about your mother, your dancing and all that stuff about your

143

dream of being in a play… but what I can say is that you were right when you said I'd leave as soon as you told me your supposed truth. God knows how many men you've brought here with the same story! I bet you don't even know what number I am in your life or even your bed. You're a slut, that's what you are. Give it to me to think that a woman who strips for money could be someone to make a home with."

At that moment, she tried to slap me. In one quick reaction, I stopped her hand, holding her wrist.

"Or are you also going to deny that I saw you at the Roma Rose?" I was holding her wrists and staring at her straight ahead.

"What do you mean?" she said, very surprised.

"Alisha, my being here today is because I saw you at the restaurant with that blond man."

"Alex, it's not what you think, my love, I swear!" she released her hands from mine and tried to hug me.

"Enough, stop lying! You're just like Rosa. How lucky was my brother not to make the same mistake as I did!"

"Please, let me explain, that man… he means nothing, please, let me explain."

"What are you going to explain? Are you going to deny sleeping with him? Can you deny it to my face?" I took her wrists again and shook her hard.

"No… I can't deny that, yes, I slept with him. I can't dammit, I can't! But let me explain, for God's sake. Everything has an explanation. Please, enough, enough, Alex!" She wouldn't stop crying, with her head down, asking me for time to explain something I didn't want to hear.

"No, you stop, Alisha. I'll explain what's going to happen… I'm going to leave through that door and you won't ever see me again. I'm going to marry Lisa and I'll return to my world, the world I should've never left. That's what I'm going to do, even if it costs me blood and tears to forget you. I swear I will do it."

"Please, let me explain, it doesn't matter if you marry your girlfriend after it, but I want you to listen. I beg of you…"

"How naive I was! Thinking that I fell for you!" I said loudly, abruptly pushing her to the bed to leave, slamming the door, leaving her whole cheap movie story to her conscience.

The following day, I visited my girlfriend.

"Hi, love, what's wrong? You seem upset."

"Nothing, love. You look beautiful, Lisa!" I said, kissing her lips.

After talking for a while, she asked me if I was still seeing the bar girl. I said she had nothing to worry. I told her that I would never in my life hear of her again, that I had finally understood how blind I was, and asking for forgiveness about that, swore she'd never hear from her. I made love to her and noticed that, even though she seemed satisfied, I felt emptiness inside myself after being with her that day. I thought that, maybe, it'd been the bad time I'd spent with that deceived Alisha. From that day on, I was determined to move on with my life, I was completely determined.

# Chapter 10

**TIME** went by and my wedding with Lisa was two months away. In the time that went by, both her family and mine were happy with our decision. My brother went back to being the same he'd been with me and my parents did too. Even though they were trusting me again, I kept thinking about that bad woman. My life inside was over, even though I hid it well. Every time I had sex with Lisa, my mind was blank. We returned to our routine. It was as if the ingredient was missing… Alisha, in my brain. As if everything went well when she seduced me; as if I depended on her crumbs to be happy with another woman. Truth is I couldn't forget her. She was still in my head, as much or more than the first time I saw her. Sometimes, I craved returning to the bar to see her again, at least for a second. But the images I had in my head of her and the guy she was screwing, forced me not to look for her. I often wondered if I'd been too hard on her, or if she actually deserved everything I told her.

I felt anxious, as if I felt bad for what I'd said. 'Maybe I love Alisha instead of Lisa.' 'She played with me.' 'I can't forgive her'. 'God knows what number I am in her life'. 'Dammit, Alisha!'. 'Damn you a thousand times!'

Days kept passing and my wedding was only five weeks away. 'I have a huge desire to look for her, know about her, make love to her again'. 'My God, why do you torment me like this?' I thought on Friday, while at the office. Suddenly, my brother came in and said:

"Hello, Alex. We need to talk..."

"Tell me, John."

"I know you need to focus on your wedding, but we need to make a decision about the company's future. We also need to ask our parents for their approval to declare bankruptcy, or as a last resort, sell," his words couldn't have been more clear and precise.

"What do you think is the best decision, John", I hoped his answer would be not to sell.

"I think that selling would be the best option. I don't think sales will go back up. Every day, fewer people tend to use our products."

"Why don't we check it with our parents and based on what they say, then we can make a decision?" Truth is, I don't like the idea of selling the factory", I said, worried.

"Ok, Alex. We'll talk to them and let them decide; after all, they own 50%", he said, as turned around to leave.

"John, can I say something…? No, forget it."

"Tell me, Alex, what's wrong?"

"No, brother, forget it. We'll talk later, it's silly."

After my conversation with John, I headed home. I made myself a drink, while I watched TV; I made myself a second drink, and upon the third drink, when my watch said 9:23 pm... There she was, I couldn't get her out of my mind! I really thought it'd be easier to forget her, after everything she said and after seeing her with him. 'I don't know what's wrong with me!'. 'Why is her damn memory chasing me?' 'This mad desire to see her is haunting me!'. 'I can't believe what she said for as much as I try.' 'Alex, you're about to get married!'. 'Don't gamble with your future, forget about her!'. 'Just accept that she's with someone else.' With that third drink, I thought of so many things! I thought in the fact that within a few hours, she would come on stage. I decided, after my fifth drink, to take a bath and go to bed. While I was showering... I saw her and I thought of the first time we made love. Well...! That she made love to me. Water ran down my back and it reminded me of that passion with which she seduced me. At one point, I escaped my thoughts and got out of the shower, ready to go to bed and sleep until dawn. I lay in bed trying to sleep, but I only managed to deceive myself. The more I tried to forget her, the more I remembered her. I jumped out of my bed eluding my deception. I put on my black suit, combined it with my tie and one of my best watches and expensive shoes. I got my car keys and as I did before... decided to impress her. Even though I wasn't sure if I what I was doing was right or wrong, I went to the bar, without thinking of the consequences that could bring. I simply couldn't bear staying at home, knowing that she'd be dancing on that blessed pole, possibly looking for her next victim or dancing for him. 'I want to see her!'. 'Damn you, Alisha!'.

'Damn you a thousand times!'. 'I can't forget you'. 'What the hell did you give me?'. 'Why did you have to appear in my life?'. That was all I had in my head as I drove. Making love to her, it was always different. I could no longer adapt to Lisa. 'You've wrecked my world, Alisha!'.

When I got there, my clock said 10:38 pm. I went in and didn't care about where I'd sit; I wanted to see her without her seeing me. Everyone at the bar greeted me, very surprised by my presence, after not going for a few weeks. I sat at the bar itself and ordered the usual. I waited for her to come on stage… 'I want to see her next victim'. 'See her silent predator face.' I watched the other strippers dance, as I had my drink, jilted by a bad woman.

As I had my second drink at the bar… her friend, Rosa came on stage. As she danced, after a few minutes into her show, she looked my way, far away from the VIP. When she noticed my presence, she gave me a look of contempt that was only noticed by me. It was like an arrow, shot with the clear intent to harm, and its aim was clearly me. I couldn't understand the reason for that look, when I should've felt offended. The possibility came to mind that, perhaps, Alisha had told her everything from her point of view, and she was just defending her friend. I didn't give her sneer much importance. I waited for her friend and her show. But instead of her, they announced Megan. It was then when I knew she wouldn't go on stage that night. Very surprised and troubled for not knowing what was happening, I went to the parking lot, trying to reach her friend Rosa and clear my doubts about what was happening. 'What the hell are you doing, Alex; just go, don't you realize she's with a different man?'. 'Forget her already!'. When I got there, I couldn't see Rosa anywhere. However, I did see her car at its usual spot, so I knew she was still inside. I waited, for about twenty minutes, leaning on her car. She came out through the door, and walked towards me with the same contemptuous look. Approaching me, and without further ado, she said:

"Stupid!", she said pushing me aside, and opening the car door.

I tried preventing her from getting on and driving away. I look her arm and said:

"What's wrong, Rosa? Why the attitude?"

"You dare to ask? You caveman!" she yelled angrily, shaking her arm off mine and giving me that look.

"I only want to know why Alisha didn't come on stage today." I asked, this time placing my hands on her shoulders.

"I'm not obliged to answer your questions. You selfish pig!" she quickly removed my hands from her shoulders.

"Of course you do! Weren't you the one who devised this whole plan against me, with Alisha, to get my money? And to quench her thirst for revenge?"

"You stupid selfish! Let me go, I'm on a hurry. Think whatever you want", she yelled, reopening her car door and closing it behind her.

"Why didn't she come to work tonight? You just stay silent...! Well, I'll say it myself, Rosa: couldn't she be with her new victim, picking the next one for her list or, maybe, planning her next strategy, as a prostitute? Oh, sorry no, maybe it's the same guy as always! The man I saw her at the restaurant with, whom she slept with behind my back; she brazenly told me. She didn't even have the courage to deny it. I didn't dream it, that man exists. You can't deny you're both cut from the same cloth. My brother was so lucky with you!" I shouted as she turned on her car engine; she intended to leave me standing there.

She got out of the car, and walked towards me.

"You stupid, arrogant…!" she accompanied that phrase with a slap I didn't see coming. Those weren't the only words that came out of her mouth; it was all part of a verbal beating...

"What's the matter with you, you bratty redhead?" I said, facing her again with a hand on my cheek.

"I told you once to watch your words when you talked about her in front of me; you and your brother are the same shit; you think everything revolves around you because you have a couple of bucks in your pockets. Alisha, there, sick, bedridden in a hospital because of your damn fault and you can only think of saying something stupid. Just hope to find a woman like that in this world. She may be a prostitute to you, but there's no woman in the world who has more courage than her, for having accepted my proposal to work as a stripper, even against her will, for the sole purpose of saving a life... her mother's. Now excuse me, I'm in a hurry, I have to go spend time with my friend, at her bedside! Oh...! One more thing, if you want to call her a prostitute, you can see her as you see fit, but I will say something I shouldn't; that man you saw with her at the Rome Rose does exist, you didn't dream it. She did sleep with him, not once or twice or three times… a lot of times. You want to know why? Because he was her boyfriend, another jerk just like you and your brother. Who since he learned of her illness, got tired of going with her to dialysis and abandoned her, impregnating someone else. The same who now returned for her, the one Alisha told you in that restaurant that night that she didn't want to see again. And you know why…? Because she wanted to be with you. She'd already decided it and was going to tell you the following day. Yes, Alex! There's a woman who's fallen for you to the bones, and I can assure you it's not your "fine" girlfriend, the one you're going to marry. Believe it or not… her name is Alisha. And about your brother John... yes, he was lucky, I confess, as lucky as I was for not accepting his proposal, or didn't he tell you?! You ass! Bye!" she stated very angrily, leaving me with all the confusion in the world.

At that moment, I couldn't stop her. She opened her car door, leaving in a rush and leaving me there standing, with more questions than answers. I couldn't believe Rosa had told me everything she did. 'Alisha is at the hospital because of me.' 'She loves me'. 'How can this be?'. Not knowing what to do, I walked to my car and even though I tried following her, I couldn't see her. I pulled out my phone and dialed Alisha's number. After such a long time, of course, she was no longer in my phone's memory, but she was in my head. On the other side I heard…: 'the number you've dialed is no longer in service.' I decided to go to the bar and Carlos about Alisha, my bartender friend.

"Alisha quit a few days ago because of her health. For what I understood, she's been admitted to a hospital", he said in hushed tones as if her absence hurt him.

Unable to find out the name of the hospital where she was, I played my last card, asking for her full name and Rosa's number. He gave me the number and, in the end, Alisha's first and last name. That was all I could get from Carlos. When I left the bar, I dialed Rosa's number, trying to get information about the hospital. After dialing twice:

"Hello!" she answered, without imagining whose number it was on her screen.

"Please, don't hang up."

"Who is this…? Oh, Alex?! Why are you calling me? Who gave you my number?", she said, more angry than surprised.

"I'm sorry for everything I said back there. I didn't mean to offend you or Alisha", I wanted to vindicate myself.

"Bye! I don't care about your explanations."

"Don't hang up, please! I only want to know what hospital she's at..." I noticed a deep silence on the line... she'd hung up.

Desperation made me dial her number several times, without success. Staying only with Alisha's full name, as my only way to look for her. Suddenly… my phone rang as I drove. I took the call, without precautions; bringing it to my ear, I answered the incoming call, assuming who may be calling:

"Hello, Rosa", I said agitated.

"Who's Rosa?" they asked.

Because of how quickly I'd taken the phone to my ear, I hadn't seen the number or name of the caller. I was able to think fast and get out of the situation, using the old reasonable doubt trick.

"I said hello, Lisa; not Rosa."

"I heard you well. Don't try to confuse me. I know you said Rosa", answered my girlfriend, quite sure of what she'd heard.

"My love, in my whole life I've never met a woman with that name. I could swear I said Lisa. Maybe you heard me wrong."

"Alex, I just hope that this time you're not thinking about deceiving me again, so close to our wedding. Don't you dare!"

"No, love, how could you think that?"

"I already had enough with the bar hooker."

"I haven't even been back to the bar, Lisa."

"I hope. I called you because you didn't tell me if you were coming today. I want to see you!"

"Of course, Lisa, I'm on my way. Kiss!" I hung up to try to think.

'Rosa has upset me with this whole thing about Alisha.' 'How can she be at the hospital because of me?' 'Why do I always have to be so stupid?' I can't believe it, her boyfriend, an ass who cheated on her.'

I went to my girlfriend's house and when I got to her apartment, she opened the door wearing a transparent blouse that exposed her sensuality. It was as if she was determined not to lose me, to fight for my love. She gave me a drink, took hers and after the first sip… kissed my lips with passion. While I responded to each of her kisses and caresses, my mind was somewhere else. We went into her room and she pushed me on the bed, undressing me. I let Lisa take control over me, hoping that our relationship would twist around, making me feel what I'd once felt for her… nothing seemed to work. Just by seeing her blonde short hair, I knew that wasn't the girl I wanted to have with me. Lisa, had full control at all times, but not my full attention. She covered my body with caresses and kisses, as I did hers. My caressed on her, where so vague, it felt like a job, like I had no choice. I tried pleasing her, for as much as it'd cost, I swear I gave her my best. We ended up having vain sex, as we'd been doing on previous occasions; no more no less. We fell asleep and when I awoke, she was still hugging me. She suddenly released my body and asked:

"Alex, why do I feel that in our recent encounters you've behaved differently? You no longer come as you used to, imposing yourself on me; now, it's all different. I miss the way you used to make love to me. Don't you feel anything for me anymore?" she said, leaving me as cold as our relationship.

"How can you say that, love, if you know I love you? You may feel that way because I've been leaving work exhausted recently. You know that my brother and I are doing whatever we can to not sell the factory. It's nothing, love. Don't imagine things" I said, trying to justify the obvious.

"Since you ended your relationship with that brat, your attitude towards me has been different. I can feel it", she said confidently, getting out of bed, very confused.

I had to convince her otherwise. Once she was a bit calmer, I left. I thought a lot about my girlfriend's claims and to what extent she was right. Even though I refused to acknowledge what I felt for the girl, part of me knew it was love, more than obsession. Alisha had invaded most of my thoughts and the best place in my heart. 'Apparently, I don't function well without her, without her smile, her eyes'. I took my phone and dialed Rosa's number again. I tried, over and over again, unable to contact her. The paper with Alisha's full name came to mind. I decided to call each hospital and ask for her, using her full name and information. I was determined to find her at any cost. After spending the entire morning asking, I finally found a hospital that said they had registered a woman by the name of Alisha Aller. I took my car keys and drove there, wasting no time, to make sure it was actually her.

After getting there and asking with her full name... it in fact, sounded like she had been admitted there. I asked to see her, pretending to be a family friend and got to the room she was at. When I tried going in to see her, Rosa surprised me as she was leaving, pushing me out of the room, without Alisha even noticing my presence.

"What are you looking for here, Alex?" she said, yelling between her teeth.

"I want to see Alisha", I answered, as she stopped me.

"And who told you she wants to see you? For God's sake, leave her alone!"

"I only want to know how she is."

"What do you want? Finish what you started?! Kill her with your words and arrogance. Well no, you won't see her while I'm with her. So the best thing you can do, is leave just like you came and never return", she said, uncomfortable with my presence at the clinic.

As much as I insisted on seeing her, Rosa wouldn't let me, and even though it was essential for me, I gave up because I couldn't make a scandal there. So I turned around and left. I went back to information and asked the person in charge if she could update me on Alisha's health. She couldn't give me more information than she'd already done. To my luck, she made me turn around, pointing at the doctor who was in charge of her care. He was walking down the hall. I took a few steps, reaching him.

"Hello, doctor. Are you in charge of the patient in room number 6?" I said, touching his right shoulder, seeking to know more about her health.

"Hello, sir", he answered, turning to see me.

"My name is Alex Brown and I'd like, if it'd be possible, to know more about Alisha Aller's health".

"Nice to meet you, Mr. Alex. I'm Dr. Martinez. Are you related to the patient?"

"No, doctor, I'm her boyfriend. I was away for business and just found out she's here; I'd like to know how she's doing. How's her health?"

"Well, sir… truth is she's looking well, but if she doesn't get a donor soon, her health's deterioration is imminent", his concern was evident.

"Do you think, doctor, that if she gets a transplant she could live a stable life?" I completely ignored any information on the subject.

"Well, you'll see, with a transplant, she could live a normal life, just like any other person. And whomever donates one of their kidneys will be able to do so too", he said, giving me a little explanation.

"Thank you so much for your information, Dr. Martinez. Please don't tell my girlfriend we had this conversation, she doesn't like me worrying about her health. I don't want to disturb her."

"Ok, Mr. Alex."

"Doctor, thanks for everything."

I finished my conversation with him. I went home, because as long as Rosa was with Alisha, my chances of seeing her were minimal. I couldn't stop worrying about her and her health. 'I think I was too hard on her, I shouldn't have treated her that way.' 'That damn jealousy blinded me.' Seeing her and apologizing for not having believed everything she'd told me came to mind; not wanting to listen when she wanted to explain about her ex-boyfriend. 'I need to go back to the hospital and see her'. 'I want to see how she is, but with Rosa there I won't be able to.' 'I can't let her die!'. 'This time I won't lose you Alisha!'.

The day went by, and without thinking it twice, I went to the hospital the following day. I walked towards her room. To my luck, I ran into Dr. Martinez as he was leaving. Not noticing the redhead's presence inside, I asked the doctor if my friend, Rosa was in there and he told me she'd be back later. I thought about my good fortune after asking about my supposed girlfriend's health. I left the doctor and rushed in to see her before Rosa returned. When I entered that room, it was as if my desire to be by her side returned. Even though she was asleep and not wearing any makeup, I saw the most beautiful woman in the world, a natural beauty. I felt my heart trying to jump out of my chest. I approached her, taking her right hand, careful not to disturb her sleep. I watched her, without her noticing my presence. In an instant, I went with my heart, which prompted me to gently touch her face. As I stroked her cheek...

"What do you want here?  Where's Rosa? I can't believe she'd do this to me. I told her I didn't want to see you, not to tell you where I was. Why did you come?" She was more upset than I'd ever seen her.

At that moment, I couldn't understand her reasons. She said things in a low tone, but I could see my presence there bothered her. She was very angry.

"Alisha, I came to see you. I want to talk to you, my love", my impulses were uncontrollable by her side.

"What do you mean love?! I'm not your love! Oh! You already forgot all the insults you said to me. How you rejoiced in each of the words you used. Your love?! After calling me a whore, prostitute and I don't know what else?" truth was, she was hurt.

"Forgive me, Alisha, please. Let me mend my mistake. You're right. I'm stupid, arrogant, I admit it. But please understand, I was blinded by jealousy. Just thinking about you with him, I felt like dying."

"I don't need explanations. Go away, please, I don't want to see you here. Get away from me", her tears told me how much she wanted me to leave.

"I know you love me." I tried to remind her of her love for me.

"Who told you that? It's a lie, I don't love you, I never have. You said it yourself. You noticed it."

"Don't deny it. Rosa confirmed it. Why are you so hard on me? I don't like you treating me so formally. I'm willing to leave everything for you, my love", I said with conviction and willing to fight the entire world for her.

"She's a bad friend. She brought you here, didn't she?

"No, Alisha, she doesn't even know I'm here. If she finds out I'm here, she would hit me again."

"Rosa hit you?!" she asked, very surprised.

"Yes, I went looking for you at the bar and she slapped me."

"Then, how did you get here?"

"That's a very long story. Now I only want to be with you", I said, taking one of her hands.

"Leave, please, and don't come back. Leave or I'll scream!" she said shaking her hand away from mine.

"But, Alisha, please, let me talk to you."

"I don't want to talk to you. Leave now!" she yelled, moving her face away from mine.

"Ok, I'm going, but I can assure you I'll be back. I want you to know that you're not going to die and that I will fight for our love."

"Go away and don't come back for me. Don't torment me anymore. Forget about me and my health, Alex. I don't want anything to do with you, remember that well, anything!"

# *Chapter 11*

**WHEN** I left the clinic, Alisha still had tears on her face and was very angry with me. 'I got to see her, God!' 'I got to touch her, and see her eyes again.' 'She looks beautiful when she's angry!' I left the hospital and as I drove, I thought about how beautiful she was. My desire to have her again revived when I saw her face once more. Being by her side was like needing nothing else to live. 'She can't die, never!' 'I need to get back her love and trust.' While I was immersed in my reflections, my phone rang, destroying all those nice things.

"Hello, Lisa", I pretended to be happy for her call.

"Where are you, Alex? I want for us to get together tonight, love; I need us to talk about our wedding."

"Ok, love; I'll come over tonight."

"I love you, Alex. You are my life. Bye."

During the time I was with Alisha, I had even forgotten about my wedding. 'It's only days until I get married'. 'What am I going to do with Lisa?!'. 'If she knew what I'm up to she'd kill me!'. 'I really feel that the woman I love is Alisha' 'I'm about to marry Lisa.'. 'What am I going to do, my God?' 'How am I going to get out of this?' 'My family would kill me if I fail my girlfriend again.' 'But I can't let Alisha get away'. 'Not this time!'

The day went by and I didn't go to work the following morning. I returned to the clinic, hoping that Alisha would forgive me. I went in, and the first person I saw was the redhead. Luckily, she didn't see me. She walked into her friend's room and I kept my distance. I stopped when I saw Dr. Martinez.

"Hello, doctor."

"Hello sir… sorry, Alex, right?"

"Yes, Alisha's boyfriend. Could you tell me how she's doing, doctor?"

"She's leaving the hospital today", he said, looking through some papers.

"That's very good news, doctor. So, she's doing better."

"You didn't know anything? Didn't you say you were her boyfriend?" he said surprised.

"Yes, doctor. But as she doesn't like worrying me, maybe that's why she didn't tell me, so I wouldn't leave my work."

"I don't mean just that", he said, worried.

"I don't understand, doctor."

"She's not leaving because she's doing well. I actually think she shouldn't leave. It'd be ideal for her to stay. Apparently, she's neglected her feeding in the last few weeks and that's lead to iron deficiency, anemia, which we are still treating."

"So then, doctor..."

"She doesn't want to be here. She can't afford the hospital, and she seems resigned to death; she's tired of waiting for something she doesn't know will ever come. Besides, you know that the expenses involved in staying here are several and she doesn't have insurance to cover them."

"Doctor, you can't let her go like that", my anguish was notable due to what I had just heard.

"I didn't decide it, she did. We're working to see how to get her insurance, but so far, nothing has worked. It'll be a matter of waiting."

"Doctor, please don't sign her release yet. Let me talk to her first, please", I ran to her room as quickly as I could.

I went in, even though I knew I'd run into Rosa, but I didn't care. When I went in, I noticed they were preparing everything for her departure from the clinic. I approached them, which angered her friend more than Alisha herself. She insisted that I leave.

"Please, I need to talk about something very important with Alisha."

"She doesn't want to talk to you. Leave."

"Alisha! I beg you, give me a few minutes. I need to tell you something", I claimed, standing the redhead's pushing.

"No, Alex. You and I have nothing to talk about. My friend already told you: Leave, please! We are ready to go. I don't want to listen to you."

"Alisha, you can't leave. The doctor says you're still not in condition to do so."

"What do you mean the doctor said? How do you know that?"

"He told me everything."

"What do you mean he told you everything?" Why would he do that?"

"Don't blame him. I assured him I was your boyfriend. He said you're leaving because you can't afford the hospital."

"Well, for your information, that's not why I'm leaving."

"Don't kid yourself, Alisha. Allow me and I'll cover the costs so you can stay here, while you get a donor. Don't go", I said, tossing her friend aside and taking her hand.

"I told you, that's not why I'm leaving. And I won't accept your money. Bye. Let it go, Alex", she answered, leaving the room.

"Don't go, Alisha, please!"

"Alex, she already told you she doesn't want your money. Goodbye", said Rosa, pushing me aside and following her.

"But, Rosa...!"

Truth is I couldn't stop her for as much as I tried. I could only leave, after talking to the doctor and promising him I'd find a way to bring her back to the hospital. I went to my office and when John saw me he jumped like a rabbit.

"Alex, what's wrong, how come you haven't been to work on time for a while? Did you forget the ditch the factory is in?"

"Nothing, brother."

"Don't tell me you're seeing that prostitute again."

"John, just because you're my older brother doesn't mean I'm going to allow you to offend her that way", I said, in defense mode.

"Ah! So you are seeing her again."

"I haven't seen her again, for your information. But that doesn't mean you have the right to offend her, every time you talk about her."

"Then, why do you defend her so much, Alex? Haven't you realized you're getting married in a few days? And besides, you're neglecting your work, knowing how the company is doing", he said, lowering my voice.

"I said I haven't seen her again."

"Sorry, brother. It worries me that you'll again fall into that opportunist's clutches."

"Talking about the company, what did our parents say about the situation?" I didn't want to keep hearing how he talked about Alisha; I'd explode at any point, telling him I loved her.

"They don't want to sell; but, they do understand that if it keeps going like this, it'd be better to do so."

"I also wanted to say, it'd be better to sell and not lose everything. If we continue like this, we'll end up with nothing."

"I think it'd be the best option too, brother, but I have one question. Why is it that you were so persistent in not selling the factory before, but now you're suddenly so determined", he said amazed.

"I noticed you were right, and if we don't do it this way, we could lose everything."

"There's someone interested in buying; but, the truth is they're not offering much for the factory. So I don't know if we should accept their offer. Although, to be honest, we don't have much choice, as nobody else is interested in buying."

"Well, brother, if there aren't any more options, and we've all agreed in selling, let's not think it twice before it's too late."

"Ok, Alex, I'll talk to the interested parties and let you know."

"Ok, John."

"Why are you so excited, Alex? And anxious?" He whispered as he left.

That night, I thought about Alisha and about everything that was happening. At one point, I dialed her friend, Rosa's number and for as much as I tried, she never answered. Days went by and my preoccupation about Alisha grew stronger than my preoccupation for my wedding with Lisa. The time to get married was getting closer. 'I need to see her and get her back to the hospital'. 'But, how can I convince her, if she doesn't even have a phone?'. I went to her house. I tried to get her to open the door, but she didn't seem to be in. I tried to contact Rosa by phone to see if she'd tell me anything. All to no avail. I returned to my apartment and pondered... 'Maybe she didn't want to open the door.'

Several days went by. When I got up one morning, my phone rang, it was my brother, telling me that the negotiation with the entrepreneurs to buy the factory was done. They'd agreed to pay the price. He asked me to come to the office to settle everything about the sale with the buyers and their lawyers and, thus, to close the deal as soon as possible.

I worked at my office and after settling the sale terms, I analyzed how to see Alisha. It occurred to me that Rosa could help me. I went to the bar that night, to see if I could somehow convince her and, with her mediation, talk Alisha into returning to the hospital. At the bar, I waited for the redhead's performance. Once she was done, I ran to meet her and waited next to her car. I saw her come out and noticed she was ready for the fight, as she yelled out offensive things.

"I just want to talk to you" I said, raising my hands and asking for peace.

"How many times do I have to tell you we have nothing to talk about?"

Like last time, she tried to push me aside to leave. But this time, I wouldn't let her get away that east. I took both of her hands with authority and said:

"Well, even if you don't want to talk, you're at least going to listen."

"I have nothing to hear. You stupid, arrogant man! Get on with your life and let us be", she said, shaking her hands away from mine.

"Calm down and listen to me, please. If you want, don't do it for me, do it for your friend. You know better than anyone that she needs to be at the hospital until she finds a donor. You're the only person she has and my only way to help her. You know that if she doesn't get that donor, she could leave a very distressing life", I explained, trying to reason with her.

"But, Alex, don't you understand she doesn't want to see you again, after all the damage you caused her, saying such barbarities? Now, you're looking for the chance you didn't give her that day."

"I know, Rosa, but I'm really very sorry. And now I just want to help her get out of this. I can pay for the hospital in the meantime. Please let me do it."

"You know she won't take your money. What are you going to do to get her to accept your help? I know her enough to know she won't accept anything from you. She's too proud to accept your money."

"But… not your money, Rosa." I said, drawing her attention.

"What do you mean with that? You want me to lie to my friend? Never, don't even think about it!" she turned around and walked to her car.

"Didn't you say you're her best friend?" I yelled, trying to get back her attention.

"Of course I am there's no doubt about it. I already tried giving her my kidney and we're not compatible. And if I had to give her my life, I would without even

170

considering it. I know that if she had to do it for me, she would. Did you forget that I said that we're more sisters than friends?"

"Then, if you're willing to save her life by offering yours, why do you reject my offer?"

"My friend would never forgive me!" she turned on her car to leave.

I, upon seeing how determined she was to leave without helping me achieve my goal, decided to play a card I wasn't sure of, but I couldn't let her go without convincing her to help me with her friend. A cry from my heart went our through my mouth...

"Well if you won't help her, I'm willing to give everything for her...! I'll be her donor!" I said, without measuring the consequences.

Upon hearing that, she got out of her car to approach me. With a surprised look, she placed her right hand on my chest:

"What did you say, Alex? Did I hear well...?" she look astonished.

"Yes, you heard me right. I'm willing to give her that kidney."

"Are you serious? Don't play with something like that, please" she couldn't believe my words.

Truth is, I wasn't even sure of the words that came out of me.

"Yes, I will, but you need to help me get her back to the hospital."

"It's not just that, Alex. You haven't understood anything."

171

"What else, if that's what she needs for a better life?"

"You could be serious with all that about being a potential donor. But the real reason why she left the clinic isn't just that..."

"What other reason could there be?"

"You don't understand. She doesn't have money for the surgery either, and that won't come from your checkbook. For you rich people, only money matters. Do you understand now?" she said, returning to her car.

"Well, you're wrong there too, Rosa. I am willing to pay for everything, as long as she remains the young and full of life girl I met. I told you… everything for her!"

"Are you serious, Alex? This isn't a game. This is serious and delicate; it's more than just words."

"Very serious, and if you really love her, you'll help me. I'm also willing to break up my marriage to be with her."

"If all of this is true, then ok! I'll help you. But, now, explain to me, how are we going to get her to accept all of this from you? How would we do it according to you?"

"First thing is convincing her to go back to the hospital. We'll make her think you found an institution that will pay for everything. As for the rest, we'll see".

"Truth is, I don't think she'll buy it, but I'll at least try."

"Ok, Rosa. Thank you very much for helping me with this. I'll call you to stay in touch. I'll arrange everything with the hospital so they'll accept her, and I'll also talk to Dr. Martinez for the transplant and explain a few things so he won't tell Alisha."

"I trust you, Alex. Don't fail her again. Please! I also want to make something clear. I'm not doing this for you. I'm doing it for my friend", she said, looking at me straight in the eyes before leaving.

"Then we're both doing it for her", I said, sealing a pact between us.

I left. As I drove, I realized the gravity of the decision I'd made and the consequences it had. Now, I was thinking that having said all that to Rosa was real madness. 'I don't know what I was thinking, but that was the only way to stop her'. 'Now, what am I going to do with my family, with my girlfriend?' 'How will I face this?' 'I need to fulfill my promise to Rosa'. 'I can't fail Alisha again'. 'That'd mean losing her forever.' 'My God, clear my thoughts!' 'Help me get out of this mess'. 'What was this thing about everything for her?' 'Where did that come from?' 'I only hope this is all your doing, Lord.' 'Don't leave me alone in this, please, I beg you.'

The following day, as I showered, I thought: 'I need to go to the hospital'. As I got dressed, I got a call from my girlfriend. In short, she wanted to remind me that our wedding was near. She wanted me to go see her, but I had to make up another lie. I went to the hospital and talked with Dr. Martinez to step forward for Alisha's transplant and to pay the hospital fees. After explaining everything, he said:

"Mr. Alex, there are some procedures you need to follow before anything. First we need to give you all the information you need to know for it. Once you make your decision, the second thing will be to take some compatibility tests."

The talk came, where I was informed of all the details. Once informed, I decided to be her donor. I kept in touch with Rosa, to know how her part with Alisha was going. She said that, even though she'd explained everything as we'd planned, Alisha was wondering about the institution that would cover all her medical expenses. However, she did think that she'd be able to return to the hospital at some point.

I received a call from my brother, informing me that everything was ready to close the company's sale. This was good news for me, as I'd promised to cover the girl's expenses, so I needed my share of the money as soon as possible.

# Chapter 12

**A FEW DAYS** went by, and it was only fifteen days until my wedding with Lisa. In those days, Rosa was able to convince Alisha to return to the hospital. She also told her a donor had come up, and apparently her attitude changed completely. Her desire to keep on living was blooming. I paid for some of the hospital fees when I got my share for the factory sale. On the other hand, Lisa was still excited about our wedding.

Mere days before my wedding, I had to go to the hospital to get some compatibility tests. I did it, without my family even knowing what I was up to. Up until that moment, only the redhead and I knew it. Not even Alisha was aware of what was happening behind her back. I confess I was a bit scared to do all that, without my family knowing the risk I was taking. But it was the only way; they would never accept such madness. I didn't even have the courage to stop my wedding with Lisa, how would I be able to say something like that to my parents? I recognize that, even though it was wrong to do all that behind their backs, I had stopped loving Lisa. It still wasn't clear if this was for the better or worse, but I knew it. I felt that the person I loved was Alisha. Even if that meant facing the whole world, I was strong enough to do it. But I wouldn't without first knowing if my kidney was compatible with the most beautiful girl in the world.

Once I was already at the clinic and having done everything I needed to, I only had to wait, to see whether or not I was the donor she was expecting. After leaving the clinic, my mind could only play with a yes or no. A part of me wanted everything to go well so I could donate; on the other hand, I wanted the opposite, due to the fear I had of confronting my family.

'What will I do it if everything goes well?' 'How will I call off my wedding?'. 'This anxiety is killing me, God!' I talked to Rosa about what happened the day of my analysis.

All that remained was waiting for the results. She, despite everything she had said before and of the slap she gave me that day, didn't tire of thanking me for what I was doing for her friend. The downside of all this was that every time she thanked me, I felt committed to the cause. It was at those times that I wanted to call my girlfriend and send everything to hell; my supposed love for her and my absurd wedding. I just wanted to run towards the woman I loved; the one that truly made me feel alive, who made me want to make love to her, over and over again. Truth is... I didn't know how it would all end. But I knew I had to take that risk.

Days went by and with them some things happened. My wedding was just around the corner. I no longer had my company and the woman I really loved was in a hospital bed, waiting to defeat her illness. My parents were unaware of my true feelings and of the whole mess I was in. Every time I thought about my supposedly last Friday at the bar, I laughed at myself. I only wondered two things, 'God, is my fate pushing me to Alisha or is it playing with my feelings?'.

I arrived at my parents' house for a family reunion, in which we'd discuss future projects. In that same conversation, my mother insisted in that I should associate with John in a business project he'd planned. At that moment, I wanted to say yes, as I liked the project, based on what my brother had managed to explain to me. Despite how tempted was, I ended up rejecting his proposal because a lot of my money was aimed at Alisha's surgery. Something that, just days before my wedding, my parents were still unaware of, just like my brother, sister and girlfriend.

At the end of our meeting, I spoke with my sister Sara, well, away from the others. I wanted to tell her everything that was bothering me. I couldn't deal with the pressure of the secret I was keeping from my family anymore. I needed to tell someone and get it all out. The person I'd always trusted the most had been my brother, John, maybe because we're men, was the reason we got along so well. But, as things were, I couldn't trust him, after everything that had happened between us. My sister, Sara, was my second choice. She was always my confidant, in some of my follies. While talking to her:

"I don't know if it's my impression, but you seem a bit concerned, Alex. What's up brother?"

"No sis, it's nothing. Don't worry."

"You seem strange. You know you can count on me", she placed her hands on my shoulders and insisted that something was wrong.

"Don't worry, Sara, it's just my stuff."

"Don't tell me… it's because of your wedding with Lisa, right? Don't worry about it brother, I'll give her a few tips so she can stand being by your side for a whole day, hahaha!" she said, shaking her head and throwing her blond over her back, to then shake my right shoulder, joking around.

"Truth is, yes, Sara. It's because of my wedding."

"What's wrong? Don't tell me you're afraid of marriage? Or worse, you want to get out", she said, standing in front of me and erasing her smile.

It was as if she was reading my mind. I looked around and saw that my mother was walking from one side to the other, while John was talking to my father, and Sara and I were talking in the garden, about twenty feet from them. The course our conversation was taking worried me, but she was leading me to my unburdening.

"Sara, I don't know what to do. Truth is, I don't want to marry Lisa", I said, in a whisper.

When she heard me, she grabbed my arm and led me to a more secluded area of the garden. She couldn't believe what I had just said.

"Brother, how can you say something like that just days of your wedding? Are you crazy?" she looked straight at me, very surprised.

"Sara, you know I'm telling you because I can't tell John, after everything that happened between us. I haven't even told all of this to my best friend Marc."

"But what you just told me, Alex, I don't know what to say. Don't tell me it's because of that girl you had an affair with a few months ago?" She said, guessing the reason for my decision, as she shook my shoulders.

"No, sis, it's not because of that", I tried to divert her intuition.

"If that's not the reason, then I don't get it."

"I noticed I don't love Lisa anymore. It's as simple as that, sis."

"Alex, the truth is that I don't understand anything you're saying. I feel that in everything you're telling me, something is missing. This table is missing a leg! Tell me exactly why you no longer want to marry Lisa. I'm sure it's because of the girl you met. So don't try to say otherwise, you know I know you well and I think you're hiding something else. I won't judge you for your decisions, but if she's the reason… I advise you to think it well before you make a decision you may later regret" she said, very sure that it was all because of the girl.

"Sis, it's not that. I just don't feel in love with Lisa. I don't love her anymore! I notice that when I'm beside her, it's more duty than love."

"Think of what you're doing very well, Alex. Because by marrying her without loving her, you'll only be unhappy and will make her unhappy along the line. If

179

you do it because of that girl you took home one day in my car, analyze it well before acting" she said, making it clear that what I intended to do was crazy.

Actually, I wanted to be more honest with her and tell her the whole story, and I was about to, but then I thought it wasn't the time or place to tell everything to Sara. It wasn't worth telling her it was all for Alisha. But even if I didn't tell her… she already knew. How could I tell her I was about to give a kidney for that girl? I left my parents' house a little worried, after having told Sara about my wedding, even though I made her promise not to tell them what we'd talked about, and, much less, Lisa.

My head was more troubled than ever. The mixture of feelings that dwelled inside me didn't let me see things clearly. The next day, I decided to tell Marc everything.

"What's up, Alex? What is so important that you need to tell me? You haven't even been back to the gym, what's up with you?" asked Blondie, when he got my call.

"Do you think we can meet today?"

"Of course, friend, you seem agitated. Where do you want to meet?"

"At the Big Forty Lounge in fifteen."

"Ok, I'm on my way."

Later, at the agreed place:

"Alex, what's wrong? You seem worried", asked Marc, seeing my terrorized face.

"My whole life is upside down, Blondie. My life is a drama", I said as we sat down at the last table in the restaurant, in the most isolated area."

"Alright, Alex, what's wrong?"

After half an hour and a few drinks, my friend knew the whole story, even some details.

"But, Alex, truth is I can't believe all of this. I know I won't be able to make you give up this crazy idea, but I do think you should tell your family."

"How can I do that, Marc? You know my mother and John, it's not that easy."

"Friend, I still think you should reconsider my advice. Don't risk your life like that, you don't have to", he insisted it was madness to be a donor for a stripper.

"I told you, don't insist on that, Blondie."

"Well, then the best thing you can do is tell your family. And on the way gather up the courage and stop your wedding. I want you to count on me for whatever you need, Alex."

"Thanks, Marc. You know? I think you're right. I can't stand this secret anymore. I promise I will try to tell them everything. But first, I need to know if I'm compatible with her."

"I know you won't like what I'm about to say Alex… but I hope you're not compatible to donate your kidney."

"I thank you for listening to me, Marc."

After my talk with Blondie, a few days went by and it was only five days until my wedding. I was taking a shower when the phone rang. I kept on taking my shower, thinking about so many things! And didn't give the call any importance. When I left the bathroom, already dressed, no longer caring about what kind of cloth, shoes or watch I was wearing, I took my phone;

the missed call turned out to be Dr. Martinez. When I returned his call, he asked me to go to the clinic to discuss the results of my transplant analysis. I went.

"Mr. Alex, I need to tell you that, according to the tests we took… you're a very healthy person and, also, are compatible to donate one of your kidneys to Ms. Alisha Aller."

I was stunned, unable to even move.

'My God!! What am I going to do now?' 'I need to tell my family'. 'But, how do I do it?'

"What's wrong, Mr. Alex? Aren't you glad about the news? You seem thoughtful and stunned", he asked, a bit surprised about my attitude.

"Of course, doctor. Sorry, it may be the excitement that has left me speechless."

"Remember, Mr. Alex, that even though you've given your consent for the transplant, you have the right to back out at any moment. You can decide not to donate if you so wish, you could even decide not to on the same day of the transplant. I just want that to be very clear", he was giving me options to consider.

"No, doctor, don't even think about it. Of course, I'm willing to do anything for the woman I love. Doctor, I beg you, let's do all of this as we discussed, with the utmost discretion. Don't let Alisha or anyone else find out, please."

"No problem, so it shall be. But, what about your family?"

"I'll deal with them. They'll be at the surgery."

"Ok."

"Doctor, when will the operation be?" I asked, hoping to have enough time to tell my parents.

"Well, now that it's all cleared and you've given your consent, I'd say in about three or four weeks. I shall inform you both about the exact day."

After leaving the doctor's office and hearing all that, and while driving, I reflected on everything that was coming. 'How can I do everything without my parents finding out?'. 'How can I call off my wedding with Lisa?' 'God, help me!' 'Light my way'. Tight at that moment, my phone rang and when I took it, I saw Rosa's name.

"Hello, Alex. I'm calling, because the doctor just gave me the good news that you're compatible with my friend and that you decided to do the transplant. He also said, it could be done in about four weeks or less. What a thrill Alex! Thank you for everything you're doing for my friend, really, thank you...!" she sounded very expressive and happy.

"Thank God everything went well" I said, in a hushed tone.

"But, what's wrong, Alex? You seem a bit discouraged... don't tell me that you're going to back out on everything you said and on your promise to give everything for her. Please, Alex, don't tell me that!" she sounded concerned.

"No, Rosa, it's not that. Of course I'm glad of being able to be a donor for the woman I love", I answered, changing my attitude.

"Oh! I thought you'd back out. I'm so happy for my friend, Alex! Thanks again! We'll talk later. Bye."

Hearing how happy the redhead was, my commitment to the cause grew stronger. Truth was, I was afraid of it all. I felt I was failing my family, my girlfriend, and even myself. 'What do I do, my God?' 'I love that woman'. 'I feel like I live for her'. I felt something for Alisha that I had never felt before for Lisa or any other woman. It was inexplicable. I only understood it was different. Something new to me. As I entered a restaurant, near my house, where I planned to eat something and think a bit about what was tormenting me, expecting the music and atmosphere of the place to relax me a little, my phone again caught my attention.

"Hello, brother. How are you?" This time it was Sara.

"Well, to be honest, not well."

"Don't tell me you're still thinking of calling off your wedding with Lisa?"

"Truth is, I don't know what to do, Sara, but I don't want to get married", I said, leaving the place and pacing outside the place.

"But, Alex, it's only days before the wedding. You can't wait to make a decision when it'll be too late. If you don't love her, tell her the truth and don't get married. I will be with you in whatever decision you make."

The trust she was giving me made me want to tell her more of what was actually happening. Marc's advice came to mind.

"Sis, there's something else I haven't told you..."

"What do you mean, Alex? Don't tell me you got the girl pregnant."

"No, Sara, that's not it, it's more serious than that, but I don't want to tell you over the phone. What's more... I don't know if I want to tell you at all."

"What do you mean you don't want to tell me?! Where are you now?" she asked, uneasily.

"I'm at a restaurant near my house."

"Wait for me at your apartment, I'm heading that way. Go up and I'll see you in a few minutes, Alex", she said, hanging up.

At that moment, I simply thought of what I would tell her when she came to my apartment. I only hoped she could understand me. Even though she'd been my accomplice in previous follies, I didn't think it'd be so easy this time, as this was the craziest thing I was going to do in my life. 'I don't understand how I could tell Sara there was something else'. 'I don't think she'll leave me alone until I tell her.'

As I was having a drink at home, pondering about what I'd tell my sister, I heard the doorbell. And when I opener, there she was.

"Hello, Alex. Now, you're going to tell me what all this mystery of yours is. You already know you can count on me, but I want to know the truth of what's happening", she said, making me feel comfortable, as she kissed my cheek and hugged me.

"Sara, truth is I can't bring myself up to tell you. But I also know this thorn is killing me. If I don't tell someone, I don't know what may happen", I said, determined to tell her everything.

"Don't beat around the bush, tell me now. You have me on the edge of my seat."

"Seat sis, please."

"Ok, Alex, please...!" she claimed, sitting beside me.

"Truth is, I don't only want to call off my wedding with Lisa because I don't love her; I'm also doing it for Alisha. I love her with all my heart, Sara. It's very different to anything I've felt before".

"I knew it was because of her. I always knew. I noticed it in your face when you told me about Lisa. But, Alex, just gather up the courage and tell her, before you both embark on this madness."

"There's more Sara..."

"What do you mean there's more?!"

"Yes, Sara. Thing is, Alisha... she's very ill and at the clinic, I just came from there. She's waiting to be operated, in three to four weeks. She's going to have a kidney transplant, which could really improve and prolong her quality of life", I said, with teary eyes.

"I'm so sorry brother, what a shame! You just have to hope everything goes well. With faith in God. But I guess she already has a donor, as she has a date for her surgery", she said, resting my head on her shoulder.

"Yes, they do. In fact... it's me", I said with tears in my eyes.

"What did you say, Alex?! Repeat that, please!" she asked, very surprised, letting go of me and getting up from the couch.

"I'm going to give her that kidney, Sara", I repeated, staring right at her, as I cried.

"But, have you gone mad?! My God, Alex! Don't play with me, brother."

"I'm not playing, Sara. I just settled everything with the doctor. I'm compatible to give her that kidney and save her life."

"React, my God! You have no obligation with her. Do you know the consequences that could bring? You're not thinking clearly. Please, understand!" she declared, sitting back on the couch and wrapping herself against my body again.

"I do have an obligation to her, because if she dies, I'll die of sadness."

"This is a madness I won't be part of, Alex. Out parents need to know this. One thing is getting married because you no longer love your girlfriend; quite a different one is donating an organ to that girl."

At that moment, she walked to the door, ready to tell them everything. Luckily, I was able to act quickly and stop her.

"Sis, please don't do this. Understand that I told you all of this because I trusted you, Sara. Please, don't tell them anything; at least not yet", I grabbed her shoulders and looked straight at her.

"But, I can't let you do this, Alex. Understand me, brother. I wouldn't be able to forgive myself", she said, with some tears in her eyes.

"Let's do this, Sara. I'll tell them, but let me think about it for a bit, and find the right time and way to do it. Please promise me you'll wait. Please, Sara. Promise me!"

"Ok, brother, you have until tomorrow to unravel this mess. But really think about it, Alex, you don't have to do it. There'll be another donor", she tried convincing me.

"No, Sara. For as much as everyone insists, I'm going to follow my heart."

"Brother, I won't insist anymore, but remember that if you don't tell this madness to our family... I will. And you better tell everything to Lisa and prevent her from carrying on with the illusion of the wedding. Remember it's only days away", she said crying, as she left my apartment.

'Why did I have to tell my sister all of this?' 'Maybe it was a mistake to tell her.' 'God, help me with my family!'

The day went by, and it was only four days until my wedding with Lisa. I hadn't told her anything yet. Hours before, I had to deal with several calls from my sister, to stop her impulse to tell everything to our parents, as that was the time she'd given me to make up my mind.

My phone rang and it was Dr. Martinez. In that call, we settled the date for the operation to twenty-one days from then. Time went by and I still hadn't made the decision to talk with Lisa, and much less with my parents. But that would change as hours went by, as my sister called me very angry, for not revealing the mess I was in, neither to my parents nor my girlfriend. So she decided to act on her own, she was tired of seeing Lisa prep everything for our wedding. She finished, hanging up, ready to reveal everything to our parents.

I went to her house, trying to gain some time and keep my sister from revealing everything. When I got there, I saw that my parents were sitting in the garden and Sara was walking towards them with a tray with coffee.

Greeting my parents, amid my agitation, I realized they didn't know anything yet.

"Sis, thanks for not telling them anything", I said, kissing her on the cheek as she returned to the kitchen.

"It's not that I haven't told them, I'm looking for the best way to do it. So… are you telling them or am I?" she stated, giving me an ultimatum, and looking at me decidedly.

"Ok, Sara. Give me a few minutes and a strong shot of whiskey", I said, looking for the strength within me.

After a few minutes and the whiskey shot, I approached them. My sister, fearing I would back out, said:

"Mom, Alex has something to tell you..."

My mother looked at me and asked:

"What do you need to tell us, son?"

"Well, you'll see mom. I don't know how to begin… truth is, I'm not marrying Lisa."

She got up from her seat, standing right in front of me and as her green eyes loss their brightness: she said:

"Could you repeat that, son? I'd like to be sure of what I just heard."

"Yes, mom, you heard right: I'm not getting married", I repeated, very sure of myself.

"Son, you can't be serious. Haven't you noticed it's only days before the wedding? Don't even joke about it! Tell me what's happening, because I can't understand it", she asked, noticeably angry, and still didn't believe what I was telling her.

Very elated, she insulted me over and over again. My sister and father could only see how my mother yelled nonstop.

"I'm sorry, mom, but truth is, I'm not getting married. I don't love Lisa anymore! That's the only truth", I said confidently, as she stared right at me.

Then, my mother slapped my left cheek and fell back on her seat, very disappointed in me. But it didn't end there. When my father noticed my mother no longer had the strength to keep scolding me, resumed the conversation and insulted me more in relation to the subject. My sister, Sara watched what was happening, speechless. After a few minutes, calmness came, easing the tide. I, at that moment, tried to walk away and finalize my confession, but my sister stopped me, looking at my parents.

"Alex, you said you would tell them the truth!"

"That's what I just did", I tried ending the conversation.

"You know that's not the whole truth. Are you telling them or am I?" she said, her green eyes firing up and on the verge of crying.

"Oh! There's more daughter?! Don't tell me my senseless son wants to leave Lisa for that brat from the bar. The one he dared to bring to my birthday. Please don't tell me, is that it?" said my mother, standing up with more strength than before from her seat, after letting down her hair which had been held up a few minutes before.

"Yes, mom. But that's not all…! It's more serious than that. You or me, Alex?"

"No, mom, there's nothing else", I said, trying to end the torment and go home.

"What do you mean there's nothing else, brother?! Mom, what's happening is that..."

At that moment, when Sara was about to tell my parents, I jumped to her side, preventing her from delving into her explanation by placing my hand on her mouth. But, for as much as I tried, she was able to remove my hand and there was no way to stop her.

"Mom, my brother wants to give a kidney to the bar girl. That's the real reason why he's not marrying Lisa."

"Wait, Sara! What do you mean?! A kidney? Explain this slowly. My son wants to give a kidney to whom?" she asked, trying to understand everything Sara had said, with tears in her eyes.

Minutes later, she explained the details, telling everything to my parents. Sara's explanations took everything further than I'd imagined. My mother fainted in my father's already weak arms, due to his age. My sister ended up crying and I... feeling guilty for everything.

From then on, everything went crazy. We had to take my mother to the doctor, and after she got better, she only repeated she didn't want me near her. Now, besides from having the love of my life at a hospital, awaiting an operation, I also had the woman I loved most in the world, my mother Margaret, in a different hospital due to a crisis I had caused. My brain was about to explode. I didn't know what to do with so many things in my head. 'My wedding is in four days'. 'God, help me make the best decision, please!' 'Shed light where there's only darkness!'

After fighting my thoughts and leaving my mother at the hospital in a better condition, I decided to face Lisa, who was still unaware of what was coming. She was still thinking about our wedding and all its preparations. I gathered up the courage, and went to her apartment. Once I was at her door, I could only think about the news I had to give her. I was sure I'd break her heart with my words. Ten minutes went by before I could knock on her door. She opened, on the second ring.

"Hi, love, how are you? I didn't think you'd come today. Don't tell me you want your last night as a bachelor? Because if that's your intention, I can't. You cheeky devil! You'll have to wait until we're married", she kissed my lips and took my left hand. She wouldn't stop talking, as we walked into her apartment.

'How the hell am I going to tell her this?' 'I have to, however hard it is, I have to tell her.'

"Guess what? For our honeymoon...; no better not, I better not give anything away."

"Lisa, Lisa, listen to me! There won't be a wedding. There won't be one", I said as I followed her and heard her speak.

"Do you think this is the best time for that kind of jokes, Alex?" She said, turning, very surprised, but still with a slight smile on her face.

"I'm not joking. I'm not marrying you. I can't hurt you like that."

"But, what are you talking about, Alex?! Have you gone suddenly mad? How dare you come to my house,

192

days before our wedding, only to tell me you don't want to marry me? According to you, to not hurt me. Are you insane?!" she said, changing her passive state to a very irritated one, letting go of my hand, slowly gaining that brightness in her eyes.

Within seconds, she went crazy, she wouldn't stop yelling me the most horrible things you can imagine. She cried in rage, hitting my chest. I couldn't avoid feeling sorry and guilty for what I was doing to her. I was trying to make her understand something no woman in the world could. Then, she decided it was enough. She asked me to leave her house, as she cried inconsolably. When she saw me walking to the door, she stopped me, standing in front of me. I could see how her white skin changed color, and how at times she tried pulling her hair. It was as if she wanted to make it longer, and rip some of it out.

"Just tell me something, Alex… you don't want to marry me because of that brat from the bar, right? I think that I at least deserve to know that. If you ever felt something for me, tell me."

"It doesn't matter if it's because of her or not. I no longer love you. I know you've noticed it", I said, trying to heal the wounds I'd left on her.

"Maybe it doesn't matter to you, but it does to me, I need to know who the man who, according to himself loved me more than anything in the world, is leaving me for", she stated, still crying, grabbing my shirt and shaking me.

I didn't have the courage to tell her the whole truth, so I kept the transplant deal out. Even though she knew who

I was leaving her for, she insisted that I needed to confirm that it was because of Alisha. After confirming what she suspected, she slapped me twice and threw me out of her house.

I called Sara, when I got on the car, after leaving Lisa shattered, to check up on my mother's health. Luckily, her health had improved. According to my sister, my mother was very disappointed in me. She said she didn't want to see me there. I tried, unfairly, to make my sister feel guilty for what had happened, for urging me to tell my mother the truth. After she hung up, due to the stupidities I'd said, I understood that the only one to be blamed for everything was me. Now, with nowhere to go or anybody to turn to, I went to the bar, where I started drinking like crazy. 'I can't even think about going to John'. 'What do I do, my God?' 'Why are you testing me this way?' Lost in my thoughts, my phone rang.

"Alex, tell me what dad just told me isn't true", said my brother, very angry.

"Yes, it is true, John. It is true."

"How can you do something so stupid? Putting it above our mother's health and us, your family. Have you gone mad?! Shit, brother, react!" he yelled angrily.

"Bye, John. I'm not in the mood for your claims or sermons."

I hung up, and still John continued calling, over and over. I didn't answer again, as I knew he'd keep on claiming for the same thing. I fell asleep, after such a stressful day.

I woke up the next morning, unable to avoid thinking about my family and how angry they were with me. I called my mother to see how she was. My sister, Sara answered my call. After a brief conversation with her, I found out that her health was much better and had gone back home. When I asked my sister to get my mother on the phone, hoping to talk to her, I heard a voice in the background:

"I have nothing to say to him, until he desists from this madness", it was my mother's voice.

I settled at least with knowing that she was ok. I felt overwhelmed and frustrated, for everything I had caused to the people I loved the most. I tried busying my mind with one of my passions, so I wouldn't think so much about what was happening... the gym. At least I could talk to Marc there.

# *Chapter 13*

**TWO** more days went by and the day of the surgery day was approaching. I was trying to convince my mother to talk to me, to no avail. My family wanted to know, each time less, about the craziness, according to them, that I was about to commit. In those days, I received innumerable calls from Lisa. Her insults grew stronger, when she found out, through my family, that I wasn't leaving her only because I didn't love her, but also because I was planning to give one of my kidneys to the stripper. Finding out about that, was devastating to her. In short, she told me she would never get back together with me, even if it cost her tears of blood.

As days went by, I only talked to Rosa and my friend, Blondie. The gym, more than a passion, became a distraction for me; it was the only place where I could unload all my frustration. I tried to talk to Alisha several times. She persisted on not wanting to talk to me. Rosa

197

and I then decided that the less I chased her before the operation, the better; as she could realize what was happening. According to the redhead, knowing her as she did, she would've preferred to die than to accept a favor from me.

Days went by and nothing changed. The day that was supposed to be my wedding day, went by like any day. Only days before the surgery, I got a call. It surprised me to see my sister, Sara's name on the screen.

"Alex, please, give up this craziness. You still have time", she said, very worried.

"Sara, if you only called for that, I want to tell you, you're wasting your time", I said, very sure of what I was about to do.

"I didn't only call for that. Mom wants to talk to you", she said, surprising me even more.

"All right, put her on the phone."

"No, Alex, she wants you to come."

"And do you know why she wants me to go?"

"I don't know, brother, she only asked me to call you."

"Okay, tell her I'm on my way."

I went my parents' home, eager to see them again. Even though I could image why my mother had summoned me, I couldn't and shouldn't refuse to see them again. I arrived and my surprise was bigger than expected... the first face I saw was my ex-girlfriend Lisa's. I felt as if my family was trying to make me feel guilty, forging a plan with her.

"Hi, Lisa, what are you doing here?" I said, surprised, not having seen her in weeks.

"The fact that you and I are no longer together, Alex, doesn't mean that I should stop seeing your family."

"Sorry, you're right."

After greeting my ex, I hugged my parents tightly. I really needed that hug; seeing my old man's white hair and my beautiful mother's wavy black hair. I continued greeting everyone, and a few minutes later, it was as if my entire family was following a pattern. They left me alone with Lisa, each pretending they had something to do.

"I want to talk to you, Alex," said Lisa softly.

"I imagined you would."

"Truth is, I'm not here by chance. My love... I'm willing to forgive you. But, please, you need to forget the madness in which you're about to embark. I still love you! I haven't been able to forget you! For as much as everything you did hurt me. I need to be by your side. Forget about that slut and let's go back to being what we always were. Please!" She said, taking my hands with tears in her eyes.

"I know what I did to you has no excuse or pardon, Lisa. While we were together, I swear I was the happiest man in the world, but now, everything pushes me to her. Even though you all think she's a prostitute, an opportunist, and other things, I can't forget that woman. I know I shouldn't be satin saying this to the woman I was about to take to the altar, but my life without Alisha doesn't many any sense," I said, with my heart in my hands.

"And you say that just like that, Alex. How cruel have you become since that… well, that brat arrived!"

"I have to be honest with you. I don't want to keep on hurting you with my lies."

"You can still back out and for us to be as we were. You could even get your family back. We'd get married, as planned. We'd only need to set another date", she was trying to convince me to return to her.

"Don't insist, please. Don't make me feel worse than I already do."

"You're a senseless ass, Alex. Once you realize you don't belong in her world, you'll come back to me, you'll see", these were her last words, before she slapped me and ran away.

While my parents and sister were still somewhere in the house, Lisa left and my brother John came.

"I wanted to talk to you, brother. I want you to explain, what do you mean that you want to give your kidney to that prostitute?" He said angrily, not even greeting me, even though we hadn't seen each over in a while.

"I don't have to give you any explanation. And I'll ask you, please, to not talk about her in that way."

"So now, it turns out that that opportunistic slug is more important than your family."

"I already told you to respect her. You have no right to express yourself in this way. Instead, why don't you tell me… what did you propose to Rosa?"

"What do you mean? Who's Rosa?"

"Have you forgotten the woman you stopped going to the bar for and the one you fought with Marc over?"

"We promised that'd be a settled matter between us and that we would never talk about it again, Alex. Besides, why does that matter?" Mentioning the past startled him.

"It turns out that she told me you promised her something you never told me… could it be marriage? Why don't you tell me about that?" I rubbed his past in his face mercilessly, even though I'd promised not to talk about it.

"So she told you? That woman and Blondie are meant for each other. Don't tell me that that bitch is your beloved friend now?!"

"For your information, she's her best friend."

"You're a…"

My brother and I started a very heated discussion. So heated, that our screams were heard in the garden. We almost ended up in a fistfight; if it weren't because my parents and Sara arrived. I couldn't stand the pressure they all had on me. After so much screaming and my mother telling me she didn't want to see me again as long as I didn't forget that girl, I decided to leave, saying:

"Even if you don't like it, my decision is final! I'm leaving the hospital's address on the table, in case you want to know of me."

As I drove home, my cell phone rang.

"Hi, Alex."

"Oh…! Hi Rosa. How's Alisha doing?" I said, calming my anger.

"She seems very excited about the operation. Her will to live is impressive. Alex, something's worrying me…

201

She still doesn't know you're the donor, and I'm afraid of what may happen when she finds out. She may think I betrayed her."

"Don't worry about it, Rosa. The important thing is for her to be well. We'll see how we fix this later."

"What's wrong Alex? You seem a bit suffocated. You didn't back out, did you?"

"No, Rosa, never."

"Then I'll leave you and I'll see you at the operation."

The day in which my life would change forever arrived. On that same day, I called Sara to tell her I'd go into surgery at any moment and that I would've liked my whole family to be there with me. I told her that I knew I was risking their love with my decision, and that if they really did love me, they could've understood my love for Alisha and be there for the operation. My sister answered that my parents would never accept that and that she was sorry for not being able to accompany me in that madness. Instead, she tried, for the last time, to persuade me not to do it. When I hung up, time went by and I waited for the process to begin.

Suddenly, Dr. Martinez came in and said someone was waiting outside to see me...

"Hi, Alex. How are you?"

"Little sis! You told me you wouldn't come. My mother, where is she?" I asked, looking at the room door.

I was very surprised to see her, since I thought nobody from my family would accompany me that day.

"I couldn't bear staying at home; thinking about what would happen to you, brother". She hugged me and kissed me.

"Thank you for coming, Sara. And my mother...?" I asked, for the second time.

"Don't worry about her, now. She'll come!"

"You really think she'll come?"

"Yes, I do, you're her favorite! Remember? I have to leave you now, Alex. The doctor only gave me a few minutes to see you. I love you, brother. Remember I'll be here the entire time."

"Thank you Sara, you have no idea how much it helps to hear that." When she left. The doctor came in and said:

"I'm going to give you a few minutes with Rosa. She wants to talk to you. Then, we'll proceed."

"Ok, Doctor."

"Hello, Alex, how are you feeling?" asked the redhead, taking my right hand.

"Calm, now that I know that my sister, Sara is here with me."

"Oh, that's your sister! I'm so glad you can count on her, Alex! I don't know her but, at least she doesn't look as annoying as your brother John. She looks quite nice... anyways, Alex, I'll leave you; the doctor only gave me a few minutes. I want to thank you again for everything you're doing for my friend. I only wanted to wish you luck and tell you I'll be here with you."

"Thank you. You know, Rosa... I appreciate you being the friend you are to Alisha. You seem more like family."

"I told you, Alex, we're sisters," she said as she walked out of the room, when she saw Dr. Martinez approach.

Just as the doctor said, he proceeded to sedate me and said:

"Just relax and remember beautiful things, you'll see everything will turn out well."

Those were the last words I heard before my thoughts flew away. I was imagining pretty things! As the liquid worked in my body, I thought about every moment I'd gone through with that dark-skinned girl. I remembered her eyes, that way she looked at me, how she danced, her way of treating me. The album of my thoughts was only filled with images of her. I didn't even notice when my visions were left behind to make way for my dreams.

When I opened my eyes again… everything was over. Even though hours went by, for me it was only seconds. The first face I saw when I woke up was that of my sister, Sara. She kissed and hugged me crazily. That told me lots of things, as I returned to reality.

"Brother, how do you feel?" she said, holding my hand.

"Well, to be honest, with one less kidney," I said, trying to be funny.

"Apparently, the kidney they got out was the most annoying one, hahaha!" she replied, smiling.

"How's Alisha?" I asked, wasting no time.

"Truth is, I still don't know. But I think it's all going well. Oh! Look, Alex, here comes the doctor."

"Hi, Alex. How are you feeling, champ?" Said Dr. Martinez jokingly.

That way in which he was greeting me already answered several of my concerns.

"I'm fine, doctor. I'd say ready for a second round! Hahaha! But, please tell me: how's Alisha? How did everything go?"

"Wait, let's move by steps. I have to tell you… that everything was a huge success. Both of you can now live normal lives."

"Really, Doctor?!"

"Yes, she's resting now. Ms. Rosa is with her right now. By the way... Rosa asked me to tell her when you woke up."

"Don't worry, doctor, stay here with my brother, I'll go tell Alisha and Rosa that Alex woke up."

When I heard Sara say that, I reacted.

"No, Sara... wait. Let the doctor do it. I need to talk to you."

"Tell me, Alex, what do you need?"

"I'd like to know if my parents have contacted you. Have they been here?"

"Truth is, Alex! They didn't want to come. You know how proud our mother is. But I can tell you they've been calling, constantly, to hear from you."

"It seems like they don't care."

"Don't say that, brother. You know how mom is and that dad doesn't take a step without her agreeing. But never doubt their love for us. You can't blame them, for the madness you suddenly came up with. Give them time, please."

"Maybe you're right. I have to tell you something you don't know yet, little sis..."

"Don't tell me that after all of this, there's more..."

"When you said a while ago you'd tell Alisha and Rosa that I woke up, I stopped you, because she still doesn't know it was me who gave her the kidney."

"But, Alex! Now I really do believe that you're very much in love or very crazy. So you mean to say that, after all of this, you don't even know if you'll get to share your life with her", she said, staring right at me and pacing around the room.

"She still hasn't forgiven me for insulting her like I did. I said very nasty things to her. I offended her in a thousand ways."

"Oh, brother! So, what's going to happen between you two?"

Right at that moment, Rosa arrived.

"Hello, how are you, Alex? Can I come in?" She asked from the doorway.

"Hi, Rosa. You know my sister Sara, right?"

"Yes, Alex, I had the pleasure. Your sister is very nice", she said with a broad smile.

"You're right; she doesn't have my character nor John's. That's why she's my little sister. I think she's the only normal one in the family."

"At least I'm not as annoying as you and John, that's enough to be normal. Hahaha! It's a joke, Alex," said the redhead jokingly.

"I know, Rosa. I just noticed it, hahaha! How's Alisha?"

"She's doing very well, thanks to you. I want to tell you something, but... I don't know if I should, in front of your sister. It has to do with Alisha and you", she whispered discreetly.

"Don't worry, my sister knows everything. You can speak openly."

"Alisha keeps on asking for her donor. She always thought the donor was a deceased person, until I told her that person was alive. She's insisting on meeting him, but there's something else, something I didn't tell you before… she asked, several times, if you got married…; she did so again today. She wants to know what happened with you. What do we do now?"

"I thought you told her there was no wedding."

"It's just that the times she asked about you, I always told her I didn't know anything, so she wouldn't suspect we were in contact and that you were the person paying for the hospital. I didn't tell you anything either, so you wouldn't go looking for her."

"I don't know, Rosa. We'll think of something."

"She's persisting to the doctor a lot about meeting you. But as he promised not to say anything, he can only say it was your decision."

"It's ok. I'll see how to tell her later. Can you give me a minute to talk to my sister?"

"Okay, Alex. I'll go see Alisha."

"Brother, does she mean you're paying for the hospital?" she asked, approaching me.

"Yes, Sara. And that's not all. I'm also paying for the operation."

"But, by God, what are you doing?! Have you gone mad?! Surprises just keep coming with you", she said, sitting next to me.

"There's more, Sara. I have spent almost all the money I got from the factory on this operation."

"You are really crazy! That girl doesn't even know what you've done for her, and look at yourself! Telling me you've spent your entire capital to save her life".

"That doesn't matter anymore. What matters now is that she's ok, and that's it", I said, very pleased with my action.

"Can you imagine when mom finds out about this? That you've spent everything you have on that girl, what will happen? Speaking of mother... she's calling! Probably to know about you. Let me answer", she said, taking her phone.

Just as Sara said, my mother wanted to know about me. But for as much as I insisted on talking to her, I couldn't. Her pride clouded the reality of the situation. But I was able to talk to my father.

"Hi, Dad, how are you?"

"Good, son, how are you?" he answered, his voice tired due to his age.

"Why does my mother persist on fighting with me? I want to talk to her."

"Son, give her time, you know her well; she's decided not to forgive this madness. But sooner or later she'll understand what you did", said my father, giving me his blessing.

I felt better when my father told me he was glad to know everything had gone well. He apologized for my mother not wanting to talk to me. He assured me she was crying at that moment, just by finding out I was well. He also said that they were both calm because they knew my sister was with me. I asked about my brother, John, and he said that even though he was glad I was well, he was still very angry with me.

Days passed and both Alisha and I were much better. According to her friend Rosa, she kept insisting on meeting her donor. So we decided to tell her everything after we left the hospital. We were both still hospitalized and I thought of something… to call Rosa while she was in Alisha's room. My sister left to get something to eat, so I took advantage of the moment.

"Hi, Rosa."

"Hi, how are you?" She said, very surprised.

"I want to know how Alisha is… truth is, I called because I want to talk to her."

"Talk to her?!" She said in a small yell that seemed to have escaped her. Then, in the back, I heard a voice say:

"Who is it, Rosa? Who wants to talk to me?"

After not hearing her voice in several weeks. I just stayed quiet and heard Rosa answer:

"It's nothing, Alis, wrong number."

"Give me the phone, Rosa. Don't lie to me! I know it's not a wrong number. You know there's no naivety in me."

"Tell her its Alex. Give her the phone. Let me speak to her, please."

"Give me the phone, Rosa!" Exclaimed Alisha.

"You're right, friend... it's Alex! He insists on talking to you!" I heard her shout.

"Alex...?!" Tell that gentleman that we have nothing to talk about.

"But, friend, talk to him! Look, he hasn't stopped calling you while you've been here."

"What do you mean he hasn't stopped calling? You told me you hadn't heard from him", they were talking among them, without despairing on the other side of the phone, I waited in silence.

Hearing that voice through my cellphone was like listening to my favorite music. As they talked, I just listened quietly. It didn't matter if she answered the call or not. I was content to hear her voice in the background; that strong way she had to express herself, the commanding tone she had, imposing on everyone else. Just by hearing her voice, I knew she had gone back to being the same as before, and that filled me with joy. They continued:

"Friend, I'm sorry, but I didn't want to worry you. He's been looking after you, believe me!"

"It's weird to hear that from you, friend, as you know everything he said about me."

"Take the phone; I know you want to talk to him too. You won't lose anything by answering."

"Okay, bad friend!"

"Here she is, Alex."

"Hello."

"Hi. How are you, Alisha?" I said, a bit fearful.

"I'm fine. Remember, Alex that I'm only talking to you because my friend asked me to."

"I understand, Alisha, thanks for answering. I just wanted to make sure you went back to being the lively woman I met and whom I'm still so in love with", I tried make her see I was still dying of love for her.

"What do you mean, in love?! Aren't you in love with your wife?" She said, surprised.

"No!"

"And you say it just like that!"

"It's just that... I didn't get married."

"What do you mean you didn't get married? Didn't you have a girlfriend and were only days away from marrying her?"

"It's a long story. I'd like for you to let me see you when you leave the hospital. Do you think you could give me that chance?"

"And according to you, why should I agree to see you?"

"Because deep down I know you want to as much as I do, so don't play tough with me. I know you've asked about me, as much as I have about you."

"You're wrong. I haven't asked about you."

"You can't deny it. Rosa told me."

"Well, she lied to you. And since when do you two get along so well? If she was always the main one to tell me to try to forget you."

"And did you manage to forget me? If you think you can tell me you forgot about me and seem sincere, I swear I won't bother you anymore..." I said, playing my last card.

"I... I don't have to answer your questions", she answered, softly, letting her fear show.

At that moment, Sara entered my room.

"How are you doing, Alex? I brought you fruit so you can eat something", she said, staring at the fruit as she approached me.

Alisha, upon hearing her voice, invited me to eat:

"Good-bye, Mr. Alex! I'll leave you to eat your fruit. Liar!" she said, hanging up.

Even though I could imagine why she did that, I didn't understand her change in attitude, as I'd already told her the whole truth. It even seemed like I'd convinced her of my love for her.

"Sorry, sis. I was talking to Alisha. She's in love with me! What do you think, Sara?" I said, with an obvious smile on my face.

"Did she tell you that? Did you tell her what you did for her?" She asked, rambling and placing the fruit on the little nearby table.

"I haven't told her anything yet. And I forbid you from telling Alisha any of this. In fact, she said she wasn't in love with me, that she didn't think of me or asked about me", I said, smiling and settling into bed.

"I don't understand then, why do you say she loves you if she didn't even tell you?" she couldn't understand my happiness.

212

"You know, little sis, sometimes you don't need the right words to say what you feel. What really counts is that I felt it: she loves me! She still loves me", I felt like the luckiest man on earth. At that moment, nothing could rob me of the joyful smile I had.

# Chapter 14

**HOURS** and days went by, and the day came to leave the hospital. Alisha would leave the following day. My departure was arranged for 2:00 pm. Before preparing what would be my departure from that place, the doctor gave me an extensive talk, telling me about the kind of food I'd have to eat from that moment on. Although my life would continue to be normal, I'd have to improve the type of food I ate, as now I only had one kidney. My sister and I were ready to leave at 2:11pm. At that moment, my best ally arrived.

"Hi, Alex. How are you feeling? The doctor said you're leaving", asked Rosa.

"Yes, we've been kicked out. Get me a date with Alisha, please. Could you do that for me, Rosa?" I said, walking with a smile on my face.

"Of course, Alex! After what you've done, you've shown you really do love her. I won't take any more of your time. I have to go see Alisha. She's sleeping and will wake up at any moment. Bye, Alex. Nice to meet you, Sara."

"No, wait, Rosa...! I want to see her!" I said, in a timid cry.

"But, Alex! It wouldn't be convenient; she could wake up at any moment."

I convinced the redhead to let me go in and see her while she slept. My sister was with me, waiting until I decided to leave. We approached her room door. We waited for my accomplice to make sure she was still asleep. At her signal, I went to the foot of her bed. She looked like a damsel. After a few minutes there, Sara and Rosa insisted that it was enough and that I had to leave. There was a moment in which I couldn't stand it anymore and I took her hand gently. Rosa touched my shoulder, afraid she'd wake up. To my surprise and everyone's... she was so asleep; she didn't even feel my fearful hands caressing hers. After so much insistence on that I needed to leave, we left. Sara, though I insisted that I felt fine, didn't want to leave me alone; so she decided to stay in my apartment for that day, to keep watch over me

The next day arrived and I had a different face. My strength, will to live and confidence were back. Alisha was leaving the hospital that same day. I wanted to see her again so much, that I only thought about her. My sister had left to my parents' house. My phone rang and I ran to pick it up, thinking it could Alisha. The screen showed Sara's name. I was surprised, upon answering the call, that the person who was speaking to me wasn't her... it was my mother.

216

She asked me to go see her. I was excited to hear from her. Although she didn't say anything else, I assumed she'd pushed her pride aside to give way to her motherly love. After receiving that call, I made another one...

"Hi, Rosa. How are you?"

"How are you, Alex?" she said aloud.

She screamed my name more forcefully than usual. I assumed she was near Alisha and wanted her to know it was me who was on the phone.

"I'm calling to know if you already left the hospital. And also if I could talk to your friend."

"Yes, we're at her apartment; but about talking to her, I'd have to ask her. She says she doesn't want to. But I'm sure inside she's dying to. Give me a minute and I'll give her the phone", she said very convinced and in a slightly strong tone of voice.

On the other side of the phone, I heard my accomplice's insistence for Alisha to answer the call. There was silence.

"Hello," answered Alisha softly.

"How are you, my love?" I said, fearlessly.

"What do you mean, your love!? Who told you I'm your love?"

"Why do you insist on hiding your feelings, Alisha?"

"You already have someone in your life. Why do you insist on chasing me?"

"I know why you're saying that. But the person you heard the other day was my sister, Sara, remember her? You don't need to be jealous."

"Who told you I'm jealous? Besides, how can I know you're telling the truth?"

"Alisha, I want to see you, I want to talk to you," I said leaving all the childishness behind.

"I'm not sure I want to see you, yet. Let me think about it at least," she said, giving me hope.

"Just thinking about it works for me. Thank you, love."

"Goodbye. And I'm not your love yet. Ok!"

I was convinced that her love for me hadn't changed. I knew it'd only be a matter of time to be together again. I think that Rosa, despite everything, had a lot to do in Alisha's attitude towards me.

With a smile on my face and the best attitude, I went to my mother's house. Upon arriving there, they welcomed me with a kiss and a hug. My mother didn't give me the best of hugs, but it was a good start.

"How are you, son?" She said in that embrace.

"I'm fine, mom. I'm glad to see you again. Also you, old man. After what I did, I feel like the happiest man in the world."

"That's what I wanted to talk to you about, son… you already did your act of kindness for that girl; now, it's time to forget about this affair and return to your life", she said, as we sat in the dining room.

"Mom, I can't believe that's why you called! How can you think like that, after how much I've fought to be by the side of the woman I love, I'll renounce to my happiness?" I said, staring right at her fearlessly.

"Son, why do you hold on to that girl so badly, if she's led to so many complications? Don't you see she broke up your marriage and made you do all these crazy things? Realize that Lisa still loves you and that you could remake your life with her. You're still on time", she said, very convinced of her words, taking my right hand on that table.

"Goodbye, mom! If this is why you wanted me to come, I'd rather leave", I stood up and walk towards the exit.

"Son, I know everything! I know you wasted all your money on that madness," she shouted, chasing me.

"Who told you that?" I was surprised to hear what she said.

"I know, that's what matters. If you continue with this madness of pursuing her... don't count on me when you no longer have any luxuries and can't meet your needs, when you're alone without a single cent." Her words were as firm as her stare.

"After the life lesson "that girl" gave me, I've learned that in life you only need to live. And that's what I'm doing! Bye, mom! And whenever your love overtakes your pride, then you'll understand why your son is finally happy."

I decided to leave my mother's house and as I was leaving:

"I can't believe you told our parents about the money" I snapped at my sister, Sara, who was entering the house at that moment.

Once I was in my car, my little sister approached me, asking me to forgive her for telling my parents about the money. In spite of everything, I forgave my sister for that. In my heart there was no room for grudges. She, in spite of everything, was the only person who was with me when I needed her the most. In my anger with my mother, I drove and suddenly my cell phone rang. When I looked at the screen I saw an unknown number; I answered the call and to my surprise...

"Hi, Alex," said a voice in a soft, incomparable tone.

"Hi, Alisha."

"Sorry, Alex. You seem a bit tense. We'd better talk at some other time", she said, trying to hang up.

Even though I answered, recognizing her voice, she could perceive my mood after arguing with my mother.

"No, please don't hang up. Sorry, love, I had a bit of an argument with my mother, but nothing to worry about. Actually, thanks for calling me. I didn't recognize the number and maybe that's why I didn't sound too expressive."

"Okay, Alex. I was just calling to give you that appointment you asked for."

"Really?! That's the best news I have gotten in days, thanks love", my mood changed within second.

"This doesn't mean I'm your love. It's just so we can talk. It doesn't mean anything else".

"That's enough for me. I'm happy with just seeing you."

"Then I'll see you at the Roma Rose on Friday, remember it?"

"Of course, my love. 'How could I forget it!' If you'd like, I can pick you up."

"No need. Just wait for me there."

'Why would she pick that place?!' 'For as much as I said I would never go back there!'

After her call, I felt like the happiest man in the Universe. 'I'm seeing her again!' 'That's much more than I expected!'

My Friday appointment with Alisha was only three days away. Since we'd arranged it, nothing could cloud my happiness. My main priority those days was for the days to go by quickly so I could see her in front of me; be able to touch her, kiss her, caress her. Just imagining seeing her again gave me goose bumps. The day arrived. I got my most elegant outfit for my date with her; a white shirt, black belt with a pair of thin fabric trousers, black shoes, a watch and a good perfume. I took my Porsche keys and wasting no time, when it was time to go to the date, I headed to the Rome Rose. (Yes, I know... the one I put in my blacklist). As I waited, my hands sweat, my legs shook and my anxiety grew. A thousand things ran through my mind, as I waited for her.

'Why isn't she coming?' 'Did she forget about our date?' I was getting impatient due to the wait. I'd only been there for ten minutes, but I felt like I'd been waiting for hours. I only had a glass of water on my table, and the waiter kept coming by and asking:

"Is everything ok, sir?"

From my table, I could see who was entering or leaving the place. Ten more minutes went by, and the door opened... a high-heeled, navy-blue heeled shoe with straps wrapped around an ankle, stepped into the place's carpet. It was as if every second became a minute.

I could scan every step she took. I didn't need to see her face, to notice it was her. Every time I'd said she looked beautiful, were short in comparison. They didn't compare with how incredible she looked that night. Light blue dress, fitted around her waist, light on her knees and with a deep neckline on. I could tell she'd been to the salon, as her hair looked a bit shorter. It was in layers, and wavy at the end. I was amazed to see how beautiful she was. She seemed to have the aim of impressing me with this new look. And before I could realize it, there she was, at my table. I didn't notice how she got so close to me. She'd asked permission to sit down several times and I was still in a different dimension. I returned to the world at which she was and helped her sit down.

"Hello, my love. How are you?" I was still dazzled by her beauty.

"Hi, Alex. You look like you've just seen a ghost! I said hello and you wouldn't answer", she said, sitting at the table.

"Sorry, Alisha, I was impressed by your new look. I didn't know you'd cut your hair, I was surprised", I said, still shocked.

"You don't like it?" she asked, stroking the tips of her hair.

"Of course I do, my love! I love it! You look gorgeous! It looks like you want to impress someone", I said, with a faint smile on my face.

"Do you really think so?! I decided to get a makeover for my new life chance, that's all."

"I thought you'd done it for me"; I said trying to be funny.

222

"Apparently, your attitude has changed a lot, Alex!" She said ironically and with a faint smile on her lips.

"I decided to get a makeover for my new life chance, hahaha!"

"Don't be a copycat", she gave me a unique smile.

"What do you say if we order something, Alisha?"

"That sounds good."

A few minutes passed and we were both ready to order.

"Waiter, please!" I shouted.

"Yes sir. Are you ready to order?" he said, approaching our table and bowing his head, to look at me sideways.

She was first to order;

"For me, the steamed salmon with vegetables. All without salt, please."

"What will the gentleman have"? He asked, while he took down her order.

"The same as the lady for me, please", I said, looking at the young waiter to my left.

"But Alex…! I asked him not to put any salt in it. You don't have to order your food without salt", she whispered, staring right at me.

"The same, please. Just as she ordered it", I repeated, paying no attention to what Alisha was saying.

"What do you wish to drink?"

"Water is good for me", she said.

"That's all. Water for both", I said, thanking the waiter.

"With pleasure. I'll bring your order in just a moment", he said, walking away after taking our order.

"Are you crazy, Alex? You're going to have your meal without salt just because I did?" she said, surprised because I'd ordered the same as she had.

"Forget that, and let's get down to business. I'm not going to beat around the bush anymore, love… I want to apologize for everything I said and for not believing you, Alisha. I want you to know that, from this moment, there'll be no other person in the world I care more about than you. That nothing I do or stop doing will make sense, unless you're by my side", I said, stripping my soul before her, in the same place that led to our separation.

"You're going to make me cry, Alex. I also want to apologize for trying to find an easy way out for my problems, using you and trying to blame you for the damage other people caused."

"You don't need to apologize, Alisha."

"Yes, Alex. I feel like I owe you an explanation. I swear that what I thought about doing with you was due to my despair, when I saw my mother dying at that hospital, and the anger I felt for the rich and arrogant people in this country; also for my boyfriend leaving, when I needed him the most. If Rosa hadn't encouraged me to work at that bar, perhaps it'd all be different today", she explained with teary eyes.

"But, my love, you don't have to do this. I believe you."

"I don't mean to blame Rosa for all of this. She's been the most helpful person, since I came to this country as an immigrant. She took me into her apartment and, although she's always worked as a stripper, while I lived with her, she never encouraged me to follow her steps, until the thing happened to my mother, Clara and she saw my despair. It took her a lot to convince me, but in the end, I had no choice but to accept her proposal and to save my situation with your money, and even though I didn't insinuate anything about money to you, due to my mother's sudden death. I never thought I could fall in love with you this way. Forgive me, please, Alex!"

"What did you say, Alisha?" I asked, pausing her words.

"Forgive me."

"Before that? I think you said you were in love with me."

"Did I really say that, Alex? I do not remember," she said, attempting to sow doubts in me, with her sparkling eyes holding back her tears.

"I'm glad you decided to work at the bar that night. You taught me to value so many things. Those little things I didn't think important until you arrived that Friday. It may seem crazy that your world can change within second. In case you didn't know, Alisha, I had sworn that that night would be my last at the bar, to marry Lisa eight months later. My world changed in a way I would've never imagined. All for my own wellbeing", I said, taking her hands.

Then, the waiter arrived with our order. The night went on at the restaurant, and we both felt very comfortable. It was a night of forgiveness, of restarting. After the dinner, she accepted my offer to take her to her apartment. When we got out of the car, I felt a strange feeling. I thought of the first time I was there. Memories invaded my mind.

"Alex, do you want to come in?" She asked, gripping the door handle.

Those words were music to my ears.

"How can I deny anything to the most divine woman in this world?" I said, following her.

"Don't be so flattering, Alex. Your compliments make me blush."

I couldn't believe how much she was blushing. I felt like now I had control over her. Every word I said or every question I asked, she answered it shyly. I wondered why she was holding back so much. I could see the crazy desire she had to kiss me on her face. I, at that moment, in front of her door, waited for her to take me as she did that first night. But, to my surprise, she didn't. I even thought she was no longer the risky, outgoing woman I'd met. I was afraid to think that her new life would change her attitude; her impetus, her madness, her imposition, and all those things that though had first made me feel like a manipulated child, later made me fall in love with her. After going through the door, I found the answer to all my questions… there, on the couch, was my accomplice... the redhead. At that moment, I gave up any chance of being with her and remembering past times. Although, on the other hand, I was glad for the redhead to be there. As if we'd been intimate, I would've had to explain my scar.

"Hi, Rosa."

"Hi, Alex. Nice to see you!" She said, getting up from the couch. The same that brought back so many memories.

"I didn't know you were here," I said, very surprised.

"I'm just worried about my friend and wanted to make sure she'd come back ok. But she never told me you'd come. I was only expecting her", she said, also surprised to see me.

"I'm sorry for interrupting the conversation. Now that you're both together and behaving, I want to ask you both... why is it that you've suddenly become best friends? When you, Rosa, was the one who persisted the most in me forgetting all about him?" She asked, leaving us speechless for a few seconds.

At that moment, I thought Rosa would confess everything. It just took a glance from me, for her not to say anything.

"The truth is that Alex convinced me of his love for you, in all this time you were hospitalized. His insistence on knowing about you, his concern for what could happen to you and not getting married because of you. Don't think it was easy for him to convince me. It was hard work."

"All this sounds really strange to me! Seeing how well you two get along confuses me", she said, looking at us.

"My love, I want to show you that I'm a different person and that I'm willing to recover your love and trust in me," I said, trying to change the subject and avoid talking about the transplant. I still didn't feel it was the right time to confess everything.

"Alex, I want to believe that your repentance and your love for me is true. But I want to ask you, please, for the moment, that we just try to heal the wounds we've inflicted on each other, to carry out this thing that's starting between us… slowly. Let's imagine this is all new to us both."

"But, my love, I'm madly in love with you, I just want to be by your side. I can't imagine a life without you", I said, reiterating my love for her.

"Give me time to think, just a little, that's all I ask, to see if this all has a future. Remember that I'm not well seen in society, due to the kind of work I've done; I'd rather be sure you won't be ashamed to walk beside me, without hiding me from society and its prejudices. I'd like to be sure that you want that, remember what your social status is and what mine is."

"I understand, my love, I'll wait patiently, I swear."

After a few hours we three shared, the night ended, and even though we didn't have sex, I felt like the happiest man in the world. I knew she still loved me, and that was the most important thing.

# Chapter 15

**TWO** weeks went by since the night we reconciled at that restaurant. Not much changed. My family was still staying away from me, except for my sister Sara. I only knew about the others through her. My brother, John was still as stubborn and proud as my mother. According to Sara, my father was the only one who half understood my decision, but my mother had still not lost the illusion that I'd leave Alisha to get back together with Lisa. Rosa continued her work as a stripper. Alisha and I proceeded better than ever, and even though we still didn't have an intimate relationship, I knew the day would come. She insisted on waiting, she wanted to make sure my repentance was sincere and that I wouldn't be ashamed of her. I didn't blame her for that, as she still didn't know I was her donor. On my part, I didn't insist on having sex, before confessing it to her.

Alisha still hadn't found a job, which I didn't care much about. With the little I had, I could help her. She wouldn't accept anything from me, but with a bit of skill, between my accomplice and me, I managed to give her some money, while she got a new job, because she didn't want to go back to the bar. According to Rosa, she promised to repay every penny she gave her. Her not wanting to work as an erotic dancer again, was something that I, personally, liked. I still had my apartment and some luxuries. Truth is, the hospital took most of the money I got from the factory sale. I didn't have a job, because I grew up among wealth and hadn't learned anything besides from managing my parents' company, in which both my brother John and I worked. Both owning 20%. My sister Sara owned 10% and my parents 50%.

One Saturday my phone rang, it was Alisha inviting me to her apartment, and that I had to go because she was planning a surprise for Rosa that night.

I arrived at her apartment, just as she'd asked.

"Hello, Alex. You're right on time."

"More punctual, my darling, than a digital watch with new batteries, hahaha!"

"You're in a good mood. Come in, sit down, she won't be long", she whispered, talking about the redhead.

As we waited for Rosa, we arranged everything; a balloon, a candle and a muffin. We were talking when suddenly, the doorbell rang.

"Alex, please, turn off the lights."

When I opened the door, we both yelled: "Happy birthday, Rosa!". She didn't expect it and cried of happiness. According to her, it was the first birthday anybody had celebrated for her since she arrived in the US. That night she was turning twenty-six. After all the tears, both the redhead and Alisha's, when she asked Rosa to cut the cake…

"I want you to do it, Alis. I'd like you to do what you couldn't the day you got sick."

"What does she mean, Alisha?" I said surprised. I couldn't understand what was happening.

"Don't worry, Alex, it's in the past", stated Alisha, leaving me in the same state.

"Sorry, Alex, I'll explain, and sorry for my imprudence", said the redhead, approaching me.

"You don't have to tell him anything, Rosa. It's all in the past", said Alisha, interrupting her friend.

"What's the big mystery?"

"You see, Alex; the day she got sick, because of everything you said to her, was the day before her birthday, and we'd planned everything. She told me she wanted to spend that time day with you, as she thought it could be her last birthday, due to her illness", explained Rosa.

"Now I understand why that day you told me that, when the time came, I'd understand your invitation. I'm so sorry Alisha. I'm so sorry", I said, hugging her and giving her a long kiss.

We then put music on and saw some pictures, after so much nostalgia and Alisha deciding we wouldn't cry that night, as it was for celebration. They cut the cake together, like sisters, and I was the photographer for the whole event. Alisha gave some cake to Rosa. And within a second, she was by my side.

"Alex, here's yours," she said, leaving a plate in my hands.

"I don't want any, my love. Thanks anyways."

"What do you mean, you don't want any? Are you going to refuse my friend", she insisted that I eat it.

"It's not that beautiful..."

"It's alright for me not to eat it, as I have to look after my health after the transplant, and I have to avoid things with sugar or salt as much as I can, but you?!"

"Don't push him so much, friend; let's just keep on listening to music and enjoy the night", said the redhead.

"Rosa, now that we're on the subject of the transplant, I'd like to meet the person who made it possible for me to enjoy how beautiful life is", said Alisha, staring at her.

"Are you still insisting on that, my friend?"

"Yes, it's something I want to thank them for personally."

"I don't know, Alis. I'd have to check with the doctor and it'd have to be him who would have to convince him to see you", she answered with a certain evasiveness.

Then, my accomplice looked at me, as if giving her an answer depended on me. Due to Alisha's insistence, a few days later, Rosa and I decided that the time had come to tell her the truth, and we set up a meeting at Alisha's apartment.

When the day came in which I'd have to confess everything to the woman of my life, I was more than ready to head to her apartment that night and tell her everything. To my surprise, when I opened my apartment door... my mother and brother were in front of it, about to ring the doorbell. I never expected to see my mother there, visiting me. I knew that if she'd come to my house, with John, it wouldn't precisely be to give me a hug.

"Hi, Mom, what a pleasure to see you again, after all this time! You too, brother", I said, kissing my mother and extending a hand to John.

"Hi, son, can we come in?"

"Of course, Mother. Come in and sit."

"Son, I don't want to beat around the bush with you. I'm here because I have a proposal for you", she said, not even sitting down and pacing around me.

"I thought your presence here was to know how your son was. If I was healthy, if anything hurt or if I needed to see you. I see it isn't so!" I said, a bit disappointed in her.

"Son, you can't fool me, I know you're not doing well. You've spent almost everything you had in that relationship you insist on having with that bar brat. I want you to reconsider getting back together with Lisa. I'm willing to give you as much money as you may need, so you can associate with John in the new company he wants to buy. What do you think, Alex?"

"What do I think? That you've come to waste your time. If you really love your child, don't even propose that I give up my happiness."

"But, what happiness, son? You've only been with that woman for a few weeks and you're almost broke. Haven't you seen yourself in a mirror? Just look at yourself, you're no longer the same."

"In the days I've spent with her, I've noticed she's my real reason to live. She's the woman I love and with whom I want to marry, to form a family and have children."

"Do you remember you said the exact same thing about Lisa? That she was the woman of your life and I don't remember what else. What tells you that it won't be the same this time?" she doubted that we could be happy.

"If you're done, mother, excuse me, but I have to go! I have something very important to resolve."

"Brother, listen to mom. She's giving you the chance for us to work together again, so you can get back all the money you've thrown away on that..." said John, touching my shoulders.

"Yes, it's true John, you're right... I only have a few dollars left and very few luxuries. I've spent all of my money on her and yes, it's a very tempting offer, working with you again! It'd be a pleasure, I confess. But the thing is it'd imply me leaving the woman I love, right?"

"Yes, you're right, son. But you'd be the same man you were before. Think about it, Alex", remarked my mother.

"I think you're right, and I should think about it. Can I have a minute?"

"Of course, Alex," said my brother.

"Thank you... when you leave, close the door behind you, please. I have to go", I said, after a few seconds.

"But what did you decide, son? Did you think about it?" Asked my mother when she saw me leave.

"Yes, I did. I thought I'd like to see my family at the church, the day I decide to marry Alisha. Close the door behind you, please!"

"I assure you, you won't marry her! I can promise you that son!" yelled my mother, as she saw me walking down the hallways stairs.

I left leaving them both in my apartment. As I was driving to Alisha's house, I didn't even think about what my mother and John proposed. I only thought that I was going to see the most beautiful woman in the world and that I'd tell her a truth she was expecting. I got there and rang the bell.

"Hi, Rosa. How are you?"

"Good, Alex."

"Where's Alisha?"

"She's in the bathroom. She seems a bit nervous. She doesn't know it was you who arrived. She's waiting for her donor. She sent me to open the door", she whispered.

We both walked into the living room and sat down on the couch. Alisha, upon hearing my voice, left the bathroom.

"Hi, Alex. I thought it was someone else", she said a little disappointed to see me.

"What do you mean someone else, my love? If it's only Rosa and I who visit you. And we're both here", I said, playing innocent.

"Sorry, Alex. Thing is the person who donated his kidney for me, told me he'd come over today to meet me. But, apparently, he won't; he said he'd be here an hour ago. What do you think may have happened, Rosa?" She asked, turning around to see her friend.

"I don't know, Alis. Maybe he'll show up at any moment. Right, Alex?" she asked, pinching one of my arms.

"Yes, darling. Don't worry. He'll come!" I said, addressing her.

"While you two talk, I'll finish cooking the fish and vegetables in the kitchen, in case the guest arrives. I'll leave you alone lovebirds", said Rosa, giving me a threatening look and a second pinch as she stood next to me.

While the redhead made dinner, we talked in the living room. Then Rosa set the table. According to Alisha, the person she was expecting wouldn't come.

"Let's eat, he won't come", she said with her head down, as she brought her fork with fish to her mouth.

"I'm sorry friend, He promised he would come", said Rosa, glancing at me.

I was engulfing my fish. Then Rosa went back to the kitchen. We were alone again. She wouldn't stop lamenting not being able to thank the person she was expecting.

"Rosa's fish is really good! Isn't it, Alisha?" I said, trying to strike up a conversation.

"Yes, very good," she said, head still down.

"My love, I didn't tell you how beautiful you look today."

"Really, Alex? You only say that because you're looking at me with loving eyes."

"You look lovely, Alisha, I mean it. I love that sparkle in your eyes, that one of a kind smile".

"Can I ask you something?" She said, placing her fork on the edge of her plate.

"Yes, Alisha. Sure."

"Did you really like the fish? Because it was fine for me with no salt, although I confess I miss salt and sugar. You're only doing it so I won't feel bad, right?" she whispered, staring at me.

"I confess, my beauty, that I also miss salt and sugar a lot."

"But you don't have to. I don't understand your determination to eat the same as I do. Do you think that will prove that you really love me?"

"Maybe... I don't know. Maybe because I'm missing a kidney, could that be?" I said, looking straight at her and taking her hands.

"What did you say, Alex?! Repeat that!" she said, very surprised.

"I said it might be because I'm missing a kidney."

Then, she got up letting go of my hands, as I got up, and stood in front of her with my hands on her waist.

"Alex, this isn't a joke, please", she said angrily, shaking my hands off her body.

"It's not a joke, love, it's true!" I said, with a serious face and still staring at her.

"My God, Alex! So... you're the person I've been expecting all this time! Rosa! Please, come! Is this true, Alex? He says he donated a kidney for me, is that true?" she looked at the kitchen, her hands covering her mouth.

"Yes, my friend, it's true," said Rosa, walking straight to her.

"My God, I can't believe it! Oh my God! How could you do that, Alex?" She said, sliding her hands down her cheeks.

"Because I love you, Alisha. Why else would I do it, my beauty?"

"Now I understand your sudden friendship with Rosa, the salt-less food and even your change of attitude." she lifted my shirt to see my scar, as she cried.

She hugged me like she never had before. She cried, kissing me endlessly. I cried with her and her friend hugged us both, apologizing to Alisha.

"I'm sorry, Alis, for having deceived you for such a long time, but it was the only way we had to save your life. I knew that if I told you, you wouldn't accept, I know you well and I know you'd die first than accept something like that from Alex."

"My God, Rosa! I can't believe this happened. This is taking me by surprise. I never expected it", she let go of my body and grabbed her redhead friend.

"But it did, Alisha. I couldn't let you go that easily", I said, approaching her body and embracing her waist again.

"Oh, my God, my love."

"If you came into my life, it was for a reason. That's what God wanted and I don't regret anything. In fact I thank Him for putting you in my way."

"My love! And all this time I've been thinking so badly of you. If Rosa hadn't insisted that I give you a chance, I would've never accepted to this date to see you again", she said, with slow kisses on my lips and wiping away her tears. All those kisses I craved since we had that date at Roma Rose. And which she withheld, out of pride. Abstaining from wanting to give me a night of pleasure.

"Fate insists on keeping us together," I said, staring at her head and stroking her hair.

"I have a question for you, Alex. So, the charity money, was that also you? And I want the truth!"

"I'm sorry, my friend. I lied about that too. He was the only person paying for each day you spent at the hospital. And not only that... he was the one who covered all of the operation expenses", answered her friend.

While she told her everything in detail, she couldn't hold back her tears and fell on the couch, with her hands on her face, drying her tears. She still couldn't believe that the kidney, with which she'd regained her health, was mine. I sat next to her a few minutes later, trying to make her understand why I did it. She turned around to see me.

"Thank you so much for what you've done for me, Alex. I have no way to repay you for this life opportunity you've given me", she glanced at me sideways, still crying.

"You do have a way to repay me..."

"How can I repay you, my love? I'm willing to do whatever you want, if I can."

"Will you marry me?"

She stared straight at me and amidst tears and laughter, said jokingly.

"You're going to ask for so little in exchange for my life? Hahaha! Of course I'll marry you, my love! Not only that, I promise I'll make you the happiest man in the world." Her emotion was more than noticeable.

"I can assure you, I already am the happiest man in the world. Besides, I have to stay as close as I can to my other kidney to be able to take care of it forever."

"I only want to ask for one thing in return, Alex."

"Whatever you want, I'll give it to you," I said, not hesitating for a second.

"I want my friend and sister to be our wedding's witness, and godmother to all the children we may have". Jokingly, I answered her question by saying:

"But... Rosa, my love?! Are you sure?"

"What's wrong with her?" she let go of my hands in surprise and moved away from me.

"If I've already given you a kidney, how could I refuse something we'd both love? Hahaha!"

"Apparently, it also took away your annoying side and only left your good mood, my love. Hahaha!" said Alisha, tapping my chest as we laughed.

"Which means by now, you'll be the annoying one, Alis. Let's see how Alex can handle you. Hahaha! And also, how will I handle you?" said the redhead, smiling, looking at us both.

After that emotional moment, hours went by and with them, all the nostalgia. Tears turned into laughter. And then suddenly my redhead accomplice said:

"Alis, I think you and Alex are looking forward to me leaving, right?"

"What Rosa? Don't say that! Stay and we'll keep chatting. I want to know more about you two and your strategies to keep me in the dark for so long", said Alisha, already with a slight smile on her lips and no tears in her eyes.

"Stop that, my friend. I'd better go. Goodbye, lovebirds! Enjoy your evening", said Rosa, walking out of the apartment.

"You're leaving, Rosa?" asked Alisha.

"Yes, because if I stay, you won't be able to have sex. And I can tell you both want to. In fact, you need to! Enjoy! Bye!" she said, turning around and with a wicked smile on her face.

"You cheeky thing, how dare you say something like that?" said Alisha, glancing sideways at me.

"Goodbye. Enjoy your reunion", Rosa closed the door behind her.

My accomplice left, stating what we'd both kept hidden in our minds.

"Alex, don't listen to Rosa," said Alisha, a little embarrassed, she looked like a different woman, not the one I'd seen before.

"Why not? If she's right!"

"And what is she right about?"

I approached her and pushed her into the wall, softly, placing both her hands over her shoulders, leaning my body over hers, answering her question and locking her between the wall and my body.

241

"In that we both want to be together, like this; that we want to make love; that we need to satiate the desire we feel for each other. Do you need any other reason, my beauty?" I felt like a professional seducer. I felt like I had the control I'd never had over her. I felt like a different man; not the manipulated child I'd always been to her…; however this all changed when he said:

"You're right, Alex. We're no longer children and what we feel isn't something we can hide even if we wanted to."

She then placed her hands on my waist and pressed her lips onto mine. I responded by gently biting hers. What we felt with that kiss was indescribable. With her hands already on my waist and kissing my neck, she slowly pushed me into the room I abandoned her at that time, ending the beautiful thing we had with my questions, despite how the story turned out to be for me. My heart was beating much faster than usual. I couldn't believe that what I'd been wanting for so many weeks, which had tested my love, was actually happening. She pushed me into the bed, where I lay on my back with my arms open. She took off her dress, to then proceed to strip me, slowly, until she left me with nothing. She took off the few clothes left on her body and jumped on mine, already naked, and began kissing my lips, passionately. As she kissed me, I seized her waist and could feel the heat of her naked body on mine. I bit her lips and she, mine, and her tongue and mine were one. We rolled over and now my body was on hers. With my hands on her waist, I turned her over and began running down her entire back, filling her with kisses and caresses, until I reached her buttocks; I squeezed them tightly, and then bit them. She turned around. I proceeded to her vagina, where she enjoyed what I did with my lips, causing her to moan. Placing her hands on my head, screaming, she told me how much she was enjoying that. Then she invited me to go up to her lips, and with her left hand, she took my penis, taking it to her vagina. As she moved my body over hers, I enjoyed her kisses. The sway of our bodies made our pleasurable twists turn to words. In another turn, she was on her knees on the bed, with her vagina clutching onto my penis. I lifted my back, to hug her, wrapping my arms around her waist. She placed her around my neck, as I felt her waist move, I clutched onto her shoulders and what we felt, at that moment, was unique. Then I put her on her stomach and inserted my sex into hers, as I grabbed her hair and she bit the pillow, asking me not to stop. My movements increased and she looked back, shouting, "Don't stop, my love, please, don't stop". I took her to one of the corners of the bed, holding her thighs and her cries of pleasure continued, this time, with proper names, as I spanked her buttocks. We then decided to go back to the center of the bed, and while she was under me, with her back against the bed, and looking into my eyes, she crossed her legs behind my back, and we both felt a unique sensation, she asked me to kiss her hard and she clung to my body, ending everything in one last sigh. We lay side by side, exhausted. Until that moment, I hadn't noticed the change in the room. There were no more newspaper clippings, trophies and the other things. Even the color had changed, from cream to light green. My curiosity to know what had happened with all of it, prompted me to ask:

"My love, what happened to the things you kept here?"

"You and your questions! Hahaha! And, what gives you the right to call me your love?!" she asked, playfully, looking into my eyes.

"Could it be how in love I am with you? How crazy you make me? Or, perhaps, it's this stubborn heart and its insistence in telling you what it feels?"

"It doesn't matter anymore. You can ask everything you want, my love. I'm yours and I want to be like this with you forever."

"I want that too, my beauty!"

"Answering your question. I put everything away because I don't want to cry anymore. Now, I want everything to be smiles for me. I want to enjoy every day God gives me; every second, every minute and every hour will be special to me."

"Can I ask you an indiscreet question, Alisha?"

"You and your questions."

"What's going to happen with you? I know you haven't found a job yet", I was afraid she'd want to return to the bar due to desperation.

"I need to try to find another job. Though I thank life for putting me in your way, due to my work at the bar, I know I won't be a stripper anymore", she said, turning on her side and kissing my chin, as she stroked my scar.

"I also thank life for your coming into mine, Alisha."

And so our conversation continued and then we had sex again; our desire lasted the whole night.

244

# *Chapter 16*

**AFTER** all the tears the smiles came. Days kept passing; then weeks and then months, three in total. In those months, many things happened. Alisha, my fiancée, found a cashier's job at a bookstore in Manhattan. Rosa, who had always been her best friend and support, continued working in the same bar. My sister, Sara visited me from time to time, and on a couple of occasions, she even hangs out with Alisha and her friend Rosa. My mother and brother still rejected our relationship, even though my father had tried to convince them that they needed to settle their differences with me and accept my relationship. Romance with my girlfriend, Alisha, was going quite well. But... economically, I wasn't doing well at all. I had very little money left, and even though she didn't know this, there was someone who did... my mother. Which is why she insisted on her proposal to make me join John in the company he was days away from buying. Every time she called, she said the same thing. One Tuesday, she came to my house. This time, her proposal went further, as she came with Lisa, my ex-girlfriend, the one I was days away from marrying.

"Hi, son, how are you?" She said when I opened the door.

"Hi, Mom, Lisa! How are you? But... what are you looking for?" my surprise was so big when I saw Lisa, I was stunned for a few seconds.

I couldn't help remembering some of the times we'd lived together. She looked beautiful… a very sexy and tight blue dress which highlighted the brightness of her blue eyes; a necklace with some precious stones shone on her neck. I was also surprised to see her now long, dark hair. Truth is, I was dazzled by her beauty. That change already told me a lot about her visit.

"You won't invite us in?" said my mother from the hallway.

"Of course, come in, sit down."

"Alex, we're here to make you a proposal. I know that your life isn't going well, even if you don't want to recognize it, but you know I'm not mistaken, son", she said, without getting angry.

"I know what you mean, mother; you've been calling me all this time for the same thing."

"It's not that, son; just listen to me. I'm going to invest a 30% with John, for his new company. I'm doing it, because if you decide to accept the proposal Lisa and I will make, that part of the company... will be yours."

"Mama, I already told you not to insist on that. I'll be fine." Lisa just remained quiet, without letting go of the bag she was carrying. It looked like she'd been shopping.

"You see this suit? It's for the day in which you decide to take over 30% of the company, so you can use it to marry Lisa", she said, taking the bag Lisa was holding and laying out a black suit on my couch.

"But I can't accept-"

"Son, you don't have to give an answer now. Think about it, you don't have to accept if you don't want to", she interrupted, trying to be kind.

"Yes, love. Your mother's right. I'm willing to marry you. Without thinking it twice", said Lisa, approaching me with that perfume I liked so much on her. She kissed me on the lips and they both left my apartment.

"At least, think about it, son, promise me you'll think about it!" whispered my mother, returning to my side and giving me a kiss to, now, actually leave, leaving that tempting decision in my mind.

'What the hell is all this?' 'I can't believe Lisa is still so willing.' 'Though it hurts to admit it, my mother is right, I don't know how to live like this'. 'But I can't back out now!' 'God… Lisa still looks amazing!' I told myself, as I stared at the black suit lying on my couch.

In my despair for how bad I was doing, I promised my mother, this time, I'd think about it very seriously. They both left a very good quality and elegant suit. It was just there, so I could retrieve my past life, according to them. I confess it was like leaving a pizza in front of a hungry bum; a candy at a preschool, or a blank check signed to the holder. In short, it was like leaving a coin in my hands, which I'd have to throw in the air to turn and decide my luck. In other words, it'd be choosing between two lifestyles: settling with the life I had, in a world which, though it pained me to recognize it, I didn't feel as my own, depriving myself of many of the things I loved... and of which I now had very few; or return to the life I knew, filled with luxuries, money and pleasures. That is, the world I grew up in, social status included.

I spent two months with that coin in my hands. Due to several factors, my economic situation went from bad to worse. I decided to really think about everything my mother had proposed, though it meant marrying Lisa, despite of how happy I was with Alisha. Lisa didn't seem indifferent to me that day; I also missed the world in which I was born and grew up. It was becoming increasingly difficult to adapt to my new life. I confess that, for me, having made the decision wasn't easy. I thought about it a thousand times. Maybe, not feeling pressured by my mother and some of the things that continued to happen in my environment, led me to my choice..., who knows... ?! Truth is, due to the decision I made, I was on my way to a church, wearing the black suit my mother and Lisa had left on my couch. I still didn't know if the decision that led me to that altar was the best one. Only time would tell. What I was sure of, was that, with that decision, I was hurting the woman I loved the most in the world... but that's life. We need to bet on life, even though it may affect our interests and, sometimes, the people we love; I bet on my happiness with her. Suddenly my phone rang.

"Alex!" said a woman's voice.

"What's up, sis?"

"That's what I'd like to know, why aren't you here yet? Don't you know in this case, it's the bride who has to keep you waiting? I'm starting to believe letting you come alone to the church was a mistake."

"For a moment, I thought it was she who was calling, Sara."

"That's enough, Alex. Don't tell me you're ditching another wedding?!"

"No, little sis, how could you think that? I'll be there in three minutes. Tell Dad to wait for me at the door."

"Okay. Alex, come already! The bride looks anxious."

I arrived at the church and thanked my father. Taking his arm, we walked from the door to the altar. Then, there we were; she and I, side by side, in front of the priest who would join us in marriage for life and until death do us part, according to the Law of God. The ceremony began and the priest, after a few minutes, said:

"If there's anyone in this church who opposes this union, speak now or forever..."

When I heard that, I turned my head and nobody said anything. I kept my cellphone with me at all times, in case she called... as nobody opposed, the priest continued. After she answered to the oath of loving me, respecting me and being with me, both in sickness and in health, prosperity and adversity, it was my turn to answer the same questions. Questions the father had already asked twice in a row. I didn't notice that, until my fiancée rubbed my right shoulder.

"What's the matter, Alex? Do you regret marrying me? You've been looking back for a while, staring at the door and holding on to that phone. It's like you're not here. What's the matter, my love?" She said worriedly. I looked at the priest and asked him for a few minutes; which he gave me. Then, I told her…

"I'm sorry, love. How could you think I could regret marrying you? I'll never regret having made this decision."

"Then, what's the matter? Look at the concern with which Sara and your father Frank are looking at us", she said, again placing a hand on my shoulder.

"It's just that, in spite of everything… Alisha, I was hoping my mother would come, that she'd call at the last moment; although my sister and my father did tell me that neither she nor my brother would come, at least, I expected it from her. Understand me, my love. For me, it's very important to have her here today. But you're right, Alisha, we can't keep on prolonging our wedding. Proceed, Father, please," I said, putting my phone away, giving up any hope that she'd come. Insisting hadn't worked.

After my emotional crisis, the wedding continued and, finally, the young woman who filled my life with happiness became my wife. My mother and John never showed up at the church. Therefore, I only received my father, my sister, Sara and our accomplice and wedding witness Rosa's congratulations. We also received my friend Marc's congratulations. He took John's place, who I would've liked to have as my best man in our union.

# *Chapter 17*

FROM the moment in which I'd wed Alisha... four years had passed. It was Friday and while I took a shower, I thought of all the things that had happened since that night, the one which, according to me, would be my last at Knights bar. I left the bathroom and looked in my closet. After a few minutes, I was wearing a red and white checkered shirt, price, $35 dollars; blue jeans, price, $70 dollars; a $ 30 belt, $80 shoes, one of my three perfumes, the only watch I had and then I took my keys... my home keys.

When I left the house I took a taxi, I stopped for more or less twenty minutes and then I headed to the Nite bar (yes, I know! The one I'd blacklisted, the one I always said I would never visit). When I got there, the same drunks, music, drinks, women and us, the waiters, created the ambiance...

"Hello Rosa, how are you today?" I greeted the redhead, as I usually did every night, when I got to the bar to take my place behind the bar.

"Hi, Alex. What did you get your beauty today?!" She whispered when she saw the bag in my hands.

I remained silent. She knew that every Friday I came in with something for my wife and that day would be no exception.

"Oh, oh, oh, ey! Scarf... apparently the man likes being blindfolded", she commented, when she looked into the bag with the Macy's logo.

"Why did you say that, Rosa?" I asked, surprised that she knew what had happened that time in the car.

"Uh, I think I screwed up because of the book." She said, and then paced without giving me an explanation of how she'd found out, arguing she was too busy.

'I can't believe Alisha would tell Rosa.' 'I thought it was something only we knew.' 'What did she mean with the book?! I thought of how little I'd liked her comment.

Yes, in those years, I decided to buy the bar I once swore I'd never go to with my wife Alisha. I bought it, after selling the few luxuries I still had and after telling my wife how badly I was doing financially.

Rosa and I, despite being waiters, ran the bar, while Alisha worked in her own dance studio, where she taught ballet to girls under fifteen. My wife was in her eighth month of pregnancy, so she was staying home. In the meantime, she'd left the dance school to one of her fellow instructors; while Rosa and I, attended the bar every day.

I couldn't believe I was going to be a dad. It was something that excited me quite a bit. Every night, I fell asleep caressing my wife's belly. I could feel our baby moving inside her. One morning, after leaving the bathroom...

"My love, what have you got there? What are you hiding?" I said, when I saw she had her left hand behind her back.

"It's nothing, love," she said, nervously.

"Let me see, my love", and among games and laughter, I was able to take a notepad...

When I read some of what was written in it:

"My love! Are you writing about your life? What does this mean?" I asked, surprised, after reading a few pages, walking throughout the whole living room.

"Yes, Alex. I want to write a book and for the world to know my story", she said, grabbing back her notes and taking them to her chest, being very jealous of what she'd written.

"If you're narrating your life, I imagine you're also talking about us in that book, right?" I asked, very curious and thinking about her friend, Rosa's comment.

"Of course, Alex. I think it could help a lot of people. I think it's worthy of being written, and for people to know that there's always hope", she said, very sure of what she was doing.

"I don't agree, Alisha. I don't want you to divulge our intimacies. I'd be very embarrassing to read everything that happened. Apparently, your friend, Rosa already read it, right?" I said, disagreeing with what she was writing.

"Are you ashamed of me, Alex? Of everything we went through? I'm sorry, then, for being how I am. I don't understand why you're always so afraid of everything and everyone", she said, with tears in her eyes due to my behavior and opposition with what she was writing.

"It's not that, my love, it's not that I'm ashamed of you, it's just that I would be ashamed to read my intimacies. I also don't want people to know what I had to go through to get here, and start pointing fingers at me", I said, sitting next to her, kissing her lips and caressing her belly.

"So you think you've suffered, Alex...? You have no idea what it is to suffer. If you knew everything I had to go through to get here, then you'd know what suffering is. I know you think you know what it is to lose everything in life, because you no longer have your luxuries and because of what we do to keep going, but you don't know what it feels like to lose a mother, like it happened to me, and then another one", she said, crying, hugging my chest.

"I'm sorry, beautiful. Maybe you're right. I'm still the idiot I've always been, when I say things."

We both ended up crying, trying to convince each other, about the novel she was writing. And so days went by.

One morning, while Alisha was waiting for me, as she always did, in front of our house, when I got home from the gym...

"Alex, my love, oh no, oh my God...!" she shouted as she rolled down the front steps.

"My love...!" I cried, when I saw her roll down the eight steps.

I ran to her, taking her in my arms. My wife wouldn't stop complaining of pain, and while she held her belly she just said:

"The baby, Alex, the baby. I dialed 911 as fast as I could, I called an ambulance."

After a few minutes, the paramedics arrived and my wife still couldn't get up from the floor, due to her intense pain. Very carefully, the attendants got her on the vehicle, where I also got on, then rushed her to the nearest hospital. While we were in the ambulance, my wife kept complaining. I tried calming her down, as we arrived; but she, sensing the worst, kept saying:

"My love, promise me that if I die, you're going to take care of our little girl," she said, as if she suspected she wouldn't make it.

"My love, for God's sake, don't say that; you'll be alright and so will our little girl", I said, holding her left hand and crying inconsolably.

"I'm sorry I won't be able to live, my love. Promise me you'll do everything you can to save my daughter, regardless of my life." her breathing gradually becoming slower as she spoke.

"Don't say that, Alisha, please. You'll be fine, you'll see."

"I want you to promise me, Alex. I also want you to promise me that if I die... you'll publish my book. Promise me, please. I won't be ok until you promise me", I felt like I had to.

"All right, my love, I promise! I promise I'll publish that book you've loved so much and that I will always take care of our daughter. But you're not going to die, don't say that, please. I'll make sure it doesn't happen, my beauty. I don't care what I have to do."

At that moment, she closed her eyes... my screams increased, when I saw that my wife wouldn't react, no matter how much the paramedics tried to wake her. We arrived at the hospital and as they were rushing her to a room, they left me outside, more worried than before. The anguish of not knowing what was happening tormented me. Time went by and I heard no news about my wife. After an hour and a half, one of the doctors approached me.

"Mr. Alex..."

"Yes, it's me. How are my wife and my daughter, doctor?"

"I'm going to be honest, sir... your wife is very ill. Right now, we're trying to do everything we can for me. Now, we'll operate her and take out the baby. Hoping to God that everything goes well", he explained, while I kept crying and lamenting what had happened.

Crying inconsolably, I called Rosa for the third time. She arrived with Sara. Later, my mother arrived with my father.

Hours went by and the doctor approached me again.

"Mr. Alex! I have good news."

"Tell me doctor, please tell me," I said, nervous and desperate.

"Your baby was taken out of her mother's womb, and she's a beautiful child," he explained, giving my soul some relief.

"Where is she doctor? I want to see her. And my wife, doctor, how is she? Where is she?" My excitement was noticeable, but so was my anguish.

"Unfortunately, Mr. Alex, she's still in a very delicate condition. She's very weak, you'd better pray to God for her. We don't know if she'll make it, I have to be honest with you. It'll all depend on your willpower and God's mercy. We're doing everything we can", explained the doctor, leaving us all in torment for not knowing what her recovery would be like.

My screams were so loud, they rumbled around the hospital. We had to get a room for Rosa in the same place, as she couldn't bear to know how badly her friend was doing and fainted in my arms.

Two more days went by. And even though my girl was born and she was truly beautiful, as the doctor had said, I continued to pray to God for my wife, as did my family, along with Rosa, who had recovered. We prayed all together, as Sara and my mother were also very shaken by what had happened. My father kept hugging me, encouraging me. From then on, we gave each other strength. I comforted my despair by watching our daughter; she was the only thing that gave me the strength to endure all that was happening. In all the drama we were going through, I noticed something was happening... my mother was growing fond of our daughter.

# *Chapter 18*

IT'S been five months since my daughter was born. Today is the day in which I have to tell you why after that promise I made to my wife when we were riding in that ambulance, I'm here, telling you our story. I know that, based on it, you can imagine what happened to my wife...

Well after those months at the hospital, praying for Alisha's health, I awaited to go in and see her... I think for the tenth time. A while ago, the doctor had told us how well her recovery was going, after escaping death yet again. Her improvement has been amazing in those months, and we're going home today. Her friend, Rosa and I have bent over backwards for her in these months, waiting anxiously for this moment.

"Alex, you can go in to see your wife", said the doctor, with a smile on his face, after giving her the official news that she could go home.

"Thank you doctor. I'll go see her", I said, smiling broadly.

I went in with our baby in my arms, while I waited for Rosa to take her best friend home.

"Hello, my love. How are you today?" I said, kissing her non-stop and holding our baby.

"She's beautiful, Alex! She's so beautiful!" she said excited and stroking her tiny face.

After spending a while watching our daughter, she asked:

"What are those papers you've been reading lately, Alex? You haven't put them down for days", her curiosity led her to ask me that.

"I'm checking our story one last time, my love", I said with tears in my eyes, placing out baby in her bed.

"What do you mean our story? We said we'd only publish my book if I died. That was your promise. You don't have to do it if you don't want to", she said surprised.

"My love, I know I promised."

"But, I don't understand why you're doing it, you're not obliged to. I wouldn't like to publish my novel if my husband doesn't want to."

"You're mistaken, beautiful. I do have an obligation and I'm very convinced… because of the promise I made to God, after making one to you. While you fought between life and death, I asked God that if he let you live, I'd tell our story…"

"I can't believe you wrote our story. What a nice detail, love! You really did that?" she said, looking into my eyes, and kissing me and then our girl, crying with happiness.

"Well, I didn't write it of course, but I did record every detail of it. Then, the writer put it on paper, with my authorization."

"Thank you, love. You're the best husband in the world."

"And you're the best wife I ever imagined. Do you know what you really are to me? My beautiful obsession."

"I love you, Alex!"

"Our daughter, Clara is beautiful, isn't she?" I said, as we both looked at her.

"Thanks for giving her my mother's name, Alex!"

"She's already been registered as Clara Brown."

"Can I ask you something, Alex?"

"Of course, Alisha!"

"If you wrote our story, what should I do with mine?" She said, with her draft in her hands.

"That'll be your story, my darling. I'd be happy to read it. I assure you, whomever reads mine will also want to read yours and get to know more about you", I said approving her novel.

"Can I ask you something else, Alex?"

"You and your questions, Alisha! Hahaha!" I said, jokingly.

"Alex! Would you dare...?"

"But, Alisha, my love. We're in a hospital! The doctor could… I don't know, anyone could come in" I stated, fearing to accept her request.

"Then, Alex… are you going to think about it and waste your time or make up your mind and use it wisely…"

# The End

# *Sorry... I forgot*

**As** you know, I married the woman I loved, in spite all obstacles. About my brother, John, I'll tell you that he owns his own company now, with my mother, thank God! He'll do well. And even though after all this time I only see him on certain occasions, as he won't accept my relationship with Alisha, I wish him the very best.

About my sister Sara, I can say she gets along well with my wife Alisha. She visits us sometimes, with her boyfriend Alan, and we have a lot of fun together.

About my ex-girlfriend Lisa, I can say that she got married, after insisting so long, with my mother, to get back together with her, even after she found out I'd gotten married, I think she got married less than six months ago. I wish her all the happiness she deserves, as I know she's a very good woman who can make any man in the world happy.

Oh yes… my mother! Well she stayed with my father, living in the same house, with Sara, where she sometimes welcomes John and his family. Sometimes also my daughter. We get along as well as we used to. Luckily, she ended up seeing everything that was good in my wife, and although they aren't the best of friends, they get along well, as much as possible. Sometimes, she visits us with my father and Sara. She loves playing with our daughter, Clara. She enjoys it a lot.

# Final Note

**I LEAVE** this written for those who will take the time to read it, you can judge my actions or learn from them. I simply hope that, if you ever need to throw a coin, you won't rely on my story, but on yours. Remember that every decision you make in life will have consequences, and until you throw that coin, and choose one of its sides, you won't know if it was the right one. I hope it'll always be the best decision for you.